THE BOAR IN THE PINES

THE BOAR IN THE PINES

Book One of a Trilogy

Jay A. Diem

SLOARIX Media • Detroit, MI

Copyright © 2026 Jay A. Diem

All rights reserved

ISBN: 979-8-9947608-0-2

Publisher: SloariX Media

Manufactured in the United States

First Edition

For my family—
my mother, Betty;
my wife, Booyoung;
and my sons, Sloan and Arius.

Without you, this story would never have been written.

To the Reader

This story is not about heroes who never falter.

It is about men and women who try—often imperfectly—to choose what is right when silence would be easier, safer, or more convenient. It is about moral restraint, accountability, and the quiet weight of decisions made when no one is watching.

The world of *The Boar in the Pines* is shaped by systems, power, and unintended consequences. Its characters struggle, fail, and endure. Faith is present here not as certainty, but as a walk—marked by doubt, conviction, humility, and the understanding that none of us stand righteous on our own.

This novel is the first step into a larger world. While this story unfolds as a trilogy, the questions it raises—about leadership, responsibility, and truth—do not end with a final page. They echo beyond this book, beyond this series, and into the lives we live ourselves.

If there is a single thread running through these pages, it is this:

Character is revealed not by power, but by what we choose to do with it.

Jay A. Diem

CHAPTER ONE
The Pines

The snow had fallen just enough to quiet the forest without burying it. A thin, crisp layer blanketed the pines of Androscoggin County, glowing faintly under the weak dawn light. Bud Day eased the old Ford F-150 to a stop at the edge of the logging road and let the engine idle down into silence. The truck—his restored '79 Ranger Lariat—creaked the way old machines did when they'd lived long, working lives. He rested a hand on the steering wheel for a moment, feeling the hum fade beneath his palm. It was cold enough that each breath fogged the cab. Good hunting weather. The kind that sharpened your mind and stripped the world down to simple shapes and sounds. Out here, Bud didn't have to think about paperwork or grant audits or the tremor in Gena's voice when she asked where he was going. Out here, there were only tracks, wind, and the slow, careful patterns of wild animals that wanted nothing from him.

He stepped out, the snow crunching under his boots. The air smelled of pine sap and distant woodsmoke from a farmhouse chimney, barely detectable. He lifted the rifle case from the passenger seat and set it gently on the tailgate. Even after all these years, opening the latches felt like a ritual—not sacred, exactly, but close.

Inside the case lay his M14.

Not the modernized, polymer-painted versions found in tactical units these days, but the original wood-stock body, dark and worn from the hands that held it before him. His uncle's rifle. Vietnam-era. Battle-proven. Bud had updated the optics with an old Aimpoint 3000—more nostalgia than necessity—and kept the weapon meticulously maintained. The 7.62 NATO round it fired wasn't perfect for everything, but it was perfect for this: a clean, ethical, one-shot kill on a Maine boar.

He lifted the rifle from the case and felt its weight settle against him. Solid. Familiar. Comforting in a way very few things in his life were anymore.

Bud slung the rifle and adjusted the strap on his shoulder, surveying the narrow path ahead. The woods were quiet, but he could read their silence. He'd grown up hunting the woods of the upper peninsula of Michigan, learning how to track deer with his brothers before any of them were old enough to truly understand what being lost felt like. Those skills transferred well to Maine—same cold, same trees, same signs if you knew how to look.

He found the first boar track not ten steps in: a broad, deep print pressed into the snow at a diagonal. Heavy animal. Probably a male. The spacing between prints told him it was moving steadily, not running, not wandering. On a purpose path.

Bud crouched, gloved fingers brushing lightly over the indentation. "Big fella," he murmured.

The kind of animal anyone else in the county would be thrilled to get. The kind of animal he sometimes gave away to local families who treated him like he was some sort of forest monk. He didn't mind it. People needed stories. They needed someone quiet to project the word steady onto.

He rose and followed the trail deeper into the pines.

This, right here—this stretch of woods—was where he felt most like himself. Not the paperwork version of himself. Not the "Senior Analyst, USDA" version. Not the stoic-husband-who-couldn't-say-the-right-thing version. Just the man who knew how to follow a trail and listen to the earth.

The prints held steady, weaving between fallen branches and patches of brown needles where the snow had melted thin. The boar wasn't far; Bud felt it more than he knew it. The forest had a rhythm when something large was moving ahead—birds went quiet, distances tightened, air changed temperature by a shade.

He walked another fifty yards before he heard it: a low, heavy rooting sound near a cluster of spruces.

Bud slowed his breathing, bringing the rifle up but keeping it tucked against his body. He moved with deliberate care, each step placed where snow wouldn't betray him too loudly. The wind shifted slightly, carrying the musk of the animal toward him. Big male, definitely.

He eased around the edge of a fallen log.

There it was.

A broad-shouldered boar, maybe 250 pounds, rooting beneath the snow for whatever scraps the ground had to offer. Its hide was dark, thick, and winter-toughened. The animal lifted its head once, grunting softly before returning to the ground.

Bud positioned himself beside a tree, resting the rifle stock against the trunk. He didn't rush the shot. Didn't have to. Hunting wasn't about adrenaline. It was about respect, patience, and precision.

He breathed in.

Held.

Exhaled halfway.

The shot rang out, echoing across the trees like a sharp punctuation mark on a blank page. The boar dropped instantly—clean, merciful, efficient. Bud lowered the rifle and let the quiet settle back in.

A few birds resumed their calls. Snow dust drifted lazily from a branch above him. Somewhere far behind, his truck ticked as the engine cooled.

He walked to the animal, placing a hand on its coarse hide. "Thank you," he said—not out of ritual, but habit. A small acknowledgment that the world still worked in honest ways sometimes.

He retrieved the field kit from his pack. He'd dress the boar here, haul the meat back slowly, maybe bring some to the Hassan family down the county road. The boys always loved the stories he told about hunting, even if Sly listened more than he showed and Arnie pretended he wasn't listening at all.

He worked in thoughtful silence, breath steaming in steady bursts. This—right here—was where he felt most whole. No memories intruding where they didn't belong. No flashes of alley dust or screams or the sickening sound of things breaking in human bodies.

Just cold air, honest work, and the comfort of knowing exactly who he was in this one narrow slice of the world.

When he finished, he wiped the blood from his gloves and stood, stretching his back until it cracked softly. The boar lay still, the morning light catching on its hooves.

Bud slung the M14 again and turned toward the path back to the truck. He didn't know—couldn't know—that this quiet morning would be the last uncomplicated one he'd have for a long time.

He only knew that, for now, the woods still felt like home.

Dragging the boar back took time, but Bud didn't mind. The weight grounded him, the exertion steadying his thoughts. Each rhythmic pull of the sled through the snow felt honest, uncomplicated. A man earning his keep in a world where most problems had lost the dignity of being solvable with effort.

By the time he reached the truck, the sun had climbed higher, tinting the ice-coated branches in faint gold. He loaded the dressed meat into a cooler in the bed and covered it with a tarp. The work warmed him enough that he pulled off his gloves and flexed his fingers, watching steam curl from his skin.

Bud stood there for a long moment, just breathing. Listening. Trying not to think.

He'd once told a therapist—one of the four he actually sat through—that the woods were the only place his thoughts stood in single file. Everywhere else they collided, crossed, tangled. But out here, in the cold, the world had fewer demands.

He climbed into the cab and started the engine. The truck rumbled awake, shaking slightly, the old metal complaining but dependable as ever. He rested a hand on the steering wheel and let the heat from the vents slowly thaw his face.

The drive back toward town was unhurried, the narrow roads lined with snowbanks and leaning pines. Bud cracked the window for a moment despite the cold, letting the smell of morning settle into the cab. The M14 lay on the bench seat beside him, secured and unloaded, but its presence was comforting. A quiet reminder that some tools still worked the way they were meant to.

As he turned onto the county road leading toward home, he slowed when he passed a familiar farmhouse. The Hassan place. A small, aging structure with a new extension on the rear, smoke curling from the chimney, and a couple of children's bicycles half-buried near the porch. He didn't see anyone outside—not unusual in this weather—but he still nodded once toward the house as if greeting someone.

The Hassan family reminded him of people he'd known long ago. The unspoken rules, the quiet dignity, the small efforts to build something stable in a world that rarely stayed still. Nice folks. Hardworking. They'd never asked him for anything besides advice on grazing rotation and how to navigate paperwork the state liked to sign without reading.

He'd drop off some meat later. Maybe check the fencing they'd been struggling with.

Simple things. Things he knew how to fix.

As he drove, he allowed himself to imagine the rest of the day: cooking part of the boar for dinner, sharpening the M14's firing pin spring later, maybe helping Sly with physics homework if the kid pretended, he needed it. Arnie had practice later, another game Bud hoped he could attend if the house felt stable enough for Gena.

She'd been good this morning when he'd left. Soft-voiced. Fragile, but steady. He prayed—not formally, just silently—that she'd stayed that way.

The cabin came into view through the trees, perched on a small rise above the road. Smoke rose from the chimney. The front steps were clear of snow. The truck tires crunched up the drive as he pulled in behind Gena's SUV.

He killed the engine and sat there for a beat, feeling the warmth of the hunt start to cool into the weight of everything else. Hunting was simple. Life inside the cabin was anything but.

Bud stepped out, closed the door gently so it wouldn't echo. A dog barked once from inside—short, alert, then excited.

He smiled despite himself.

When he opened the front door, the smell of coffee greeted him. The dog—a wiry mutt with too much enthusiasm and not enough coordination—bounded toward him, tail slapping wildly. Bud crouched and rubbed its ears.

"Hey, Moose," he murmured. "Good boy."

From the kitchen, he heard pans clinking. Then Gena's voice—

"Bud? That you?"

He stood, brushing snow off his coat. "Yeah. Brought back a big one."

She appeared in the doorway wearing a thick sweater and leggings, hair pulled into a loose knot. Beautiful, even tired. But there was something behind her eyes—an uncertainty that never fully left anymore.

"You're back early," she said softly.

"I got lucky." He tried a gentle smile. "Thought I'd cook some of the boar tonight."

She nodded but didn't quite meet his gaze. "Okay. The boys will like that."

He stepped forward, leaning in to kiss her cheek. She almost flinched—not away, but inward, as if bracing for something only she could feel. He rested his hand lightly on her shoulder for a moment, then let it fall.

"You sleep okay?" he asked.

She hesitated. "Mostly."

He nodded. He didn't press. Pressing never helped.

From upstairs came the sound of footsteps—one heavy, one lighter—followed by Arnie's unmistakable voice yelling something triumphant about "absolutely crushing a power play." Sly corrected him immediately with a lecture about defensive zone coverage.

Bud exhaled a quiet laugh.

Gena watched him with a softness he didn't often notice anymore. "They missed you this morning."

He brushed a hand across the back of his neck. "Missed them too."

Moose nosed his leg, impatient for attention. Bud scratched the dog's head again.

"I'm going to unload the truck," he said. "You want some coffee?"

Gena nodded. "I'll pour you a cup."

Her voice was calm. Too calm. The kind of calm that came from exhaustion, not rest. He caught the tremor in her hand as she reached for a mug and something inside him tightened.

He wanted to ask. He didn't. He wanted to fix. He couldn't. He wanted peace. But peace required both of them, and she had storms he couldn't enter without sinking.

So he stepped back into the cold, closing the door behind him gently.

The woods were quiet again. Too quiet. The kind of quiet you only noticed after leaving someplace warm.

Bud paused at the tailgate, hands resting on the edge. The air hit him harder now, colder than before, sharper. He looked back toward the cabin—the smoke curling upward, the dog pacing in the window, Gena's silhouette moving in the kitchen.

Something was shifting. He didn't know what yet. Only that he could feel the ground beginning to move beneath the surface of their lives.

But he took a breath. Lifted the cooler from the truck. And carried the weight the way he always did— one step at a time.

CHAPTER TWO
Fault Lines

The cabin felt warmer than usual when Bud stepped back inside, his arms aching pleasantly from hauling the cooler. He set it beside the door, stomped snow from his boots, and hung up his coat. The dog nudged him again, tail wagging so hard it smacked the wall.

Gena had poured him a mug of coffee and set it on the counter with the kind of precision she used when she was trying to keep her hands from shaking. The steam curled into the air, carrying the earthy scent of the dark roast she brewed in winter.

"Thanks," he said softly.

She nodded without looking up, focusing on slicing a loaf of bread. Her motions were neat, almost mechanical. Bud took his coffee and leaned against the counter across from her.

She didn't speak right away. Neither did he.

Bud sipped the coffee, letting the heat warm his throat. Gena finished slicing and pushed the bread into the toaster, fingers hovering a moment too long before stepping back. She drew in a slow breath.

"Did you sleep at all last night?" Bud asked gently.

Gena's jaw tightened. "A little."

He didn't need more than the glance she gave him to know the truth. Sleep had become rare for her. When it did come, it came in shallow, fragile waves that shattered if he shifted in the bed or breathed too loudly.

"You had a nightmare again?" he asked.

She kept her eyes on the toaster. "I don't want to talk about that right now."

He nodded. Conversations like this had a way of turning to ash between them. He didn't push her. He didn't know how anymore.

Upstairs, the boys thundered around, arguing over who had stolen whose socks. Gena flinched at the sudden burst of noise. Bud saw it and kept his face neutral.

"Arnie's game is at three," she said after a moment.

Bud smiled faintly. "Yeah? Think he'll get another one like last week?"

"He believes he will," she said, a hint of warmth cutting through the fatigue. "He's been practicing that ridiculous backhand in the driveway."

"That backhand beat a goalie twice his size," Bud said.

"It also hit me in the shin," she replied dryly.

He chuckled once. The toaster clicked, ejecting lightly browned slices. Gena buttered them quickly, then slid two onto a plate and pushed it toward him.

"You need to eat," she said.

Bud broke a piece and popped it into his mouth. He didn't realize how hungry he was until the warmth settled in his chest.

"You going to be okay today?" he asked softly.

Gena paused. Her fingers tightened on the knife.

She blinked once. Twice.

And he saw it—the subtle shift from "just tired" to that trembling, precarious edge she lived on. The one she worked hard to hide. The one he pretended not to notice because acknowledging it too directly only made her feel cornered.

"I'll try," she whispered. "It's just… some days, Bud, the edges feel too close."

He set the toast down and stepped closer. "Then we pull them back together. One piece at a time."

Her lower lip trembled. She swallowed hard.

"That sounds easy when you say it."

"It's not," he said. "Nothing about this is easy."

She looked up at him, eyes reflecting the same fear she'd worn for months now—the fear that she was not enough, that she was breaking, that she was letting him down. None of which he believed. All of which she did.

"I know," she whispered.

The boys barreled into the kitchen before either of them could say more. Sly, lanky and serious, wearing two mismatched socks. Arnie, built like a linebacker, carrying a hockey stick despite being indoors.

"Dad!" Arnie said, his face lighting up. "Did you get one today?"

"Big one," Bud said, holding his hands out in a rough approximation of the boar's size.

Arnie whistled. "Whoa. Did you use the old rifle?"

"Always," Bud said.

Sly adjusted his glasses. "Did you weigh it?"

Bud chuckled. "Didn't have time. But I'll process it later. Maybe you two can help."

Arnie grinned. Sly pretended not to care, but Bud saw the spark of interest in his eyes.

Gena offered the boys breakfast, but neither slowed down. Arnie tapped his stick on the floor. "Coach says I need to work on my first stride. You wanna help later, Dad?"

Bud nodded. "After lunch."

Arnie pumped a fist and bolted out of the room. Sly followed him, shaking his head at his brother's enthusiasm.

The kitchen fell quiet again.

Gena wiped her hands on a towel. "I think I'll go lie down for a bit."

"You want anything before you go?" Bud asked.

She hesitated. "No. I'll be fine."

She wasn't. They both knew it. But she needed the illusion of fine as much as he needed to let her have it.

As she turned to go, he reached out and touched her arm gently. She froze but didn't pull away.

"I'm here," he said softly.

Her eyes shimmered, just for a moment. Then she nodded and slipped away.

Bud stood there, holding the cooling mug, listening to her footsteps fade upstairs. The dog nudged his leg again, whining as if sensing something in the tension.

"Yeah, buddy," Bud murmured, scratching behind the dog's ear. "I know."

He poured himself another cup of coffee and walked to the sliding glass doors overlooking the woods. The morning sun cut thin beams through the branches. His mind drifted to the forest again, the silence, the ritual. It always felt wrong to leave that behind. Like stepping out of a place he belonged and into one where he was improvising every move.

He took a long sip, letting the bitterness anchor him.

Today would require steady hands. And patience. More than usual.

He took the trash out, checked the truck, and stacked fresh wood by the fireplace. Small tasks that grounded him, gave him a sense of control—control that had become a precious commodity in this house.

By noon, Gena hadn't come back downstairs.

The boys were in the living room—Sly reading something about biomechanics, Arnie watching old Bruins highlights—when Bud called up the staircase softly.

"Gena? You okay?"

A beat. Then her voice, thin but steady enough:

"I'll be fine. Just need a few more minutes."

Bud didn't press. He turned to the boys.

"You two get ready soon," he said. "We're leaving for the rink in an hour."

Arnie jumped up. "Can Moose come?"

"Only if he learns to skate," Bud said.

Arnie grinned. Sly shook his head again, but this time he smiled.

Bud checked his watch. The rink was twenty minutes away. They'd beat traffic if they left early. He walked back to the kitchen and poured out the last of the coffee.

The day was getting away from him already.

He needed to get the meat stored properly. Needed to check tomorrow's appointments. Needed to find the right words for Gena—words that didn't exist, or maybe they existed but he'd forgotten them somewhere between Mogadishu and here. Somewhere between who he'd been and who he'd become.

He washed the mug. Set it carefully on the drying rack.

The cabin creaked in the wind, a familiar sound.

Somewhere deep in his chest, Bud felt the very first hint—the faintest tremor—of the ground shifting beneath him.

But he didn't name it yet.

Didn't allow himself to.

He grabbed his coat and called upstairs again, more gently this time:

"Gena? We need to leave soon. The boys are ready."

There was a pause, then the quiet sound of her stepping out of the bedroom.

"Okay," she said weakly. "I'm coming."

Bud nodded, even though she couldn't see him.

He hoped today wouldn't break her.

He hoped he could hold the seams together long enough to get through the game.

He hoped—but hope was fragile. And they were walking on its thinnest edge.

CHAPTER THREE
Thin Ice

The Androscoggin Ice Arena smelled like sharpened steel, cold air, and a childhood Bud sometimes wished he remembered more clearly. The fluorescent lights above the rink hummed faintly, casting a washed-out glow over families sliding into wooden bleachers and kids stomping their skates against rubber mats.

Arnie's team—The Auburn Bears—swarmed the ice during warmups, smacking pucks off the boards and shouting to each other with the kind of confidence Bud wished he had bottled for emergencies.

Sly sat next to him in the bleachers, an anatomy textbook open on his lap even though Bud doubted he was actually reading it. He always carried a book during Arnie's games, a kind of intellectual security blanket.

Gena sat on Bud's other side, hands clasped tightly in her lap. She wore a heavy wool coat despite the rink's relative warmth and had pulled her scarf up high, as if she wanted to hide behind it. Her eyes darted between the ice and the crowd, never settling.

Bud took note of her breathing—shallow, not quite panicked, but strained. He lightly brushed his thumb over the back of her hand. She didn't pull away.

"Arnie's really been working hard," Bud said softly. "Coach says he's improving faster than most kids his age."

Gena attempted a smile. "He's always strong on skates."

"Strong everywhere," Bud murmured.

On the ice, Arnie took a shot from the top of the circle. The puck clanged off the bar and into the net. He looked up immediately, searching for Bud in the stands. Bud lifted a hand. Arnie grinned.

The smile vanished quickly. Sly leaned in, whispering, "His first stride is still slow, but his core rotation is better."

Bud raised an eyebrow. "Core rotation?"

Sly shrugged. "Physics applies everywhere."

Gena gave a small, brittle laugh. Bud noticed how forced it sounded.

The buzzer sounded warmups' end, and the boys skated to the bench.

Parents shifted, kids in coats raced up and down the aisle, the lights dimmed one degree as the PA system crackled to life.

Bud inhaled deeply, letting the cold nudge the edges of his mind into clarity. The rink was one of the few public places where he felt relatively at ease—noise that wasn't threatening, movement with predictable rhythms, lines of sight he could manage.

Beside him, though, Gena was drifting in the opposite direction. Her leg bounced. Her fingers tapped against her knee. Her eyes were too bright, as if reflecting something only she could see.

"You okay?" Bud whispered.

She swallowed. "Just… a lot of people."

"There always are," he said gently.

She nodded, though the look in her eyes said she wasn't convinced.

The puck dropped for the first period. The game found its rhythm quickly—two evenly matched teams trading early shots. Bud leaned forward, elbows on his knees, watching Arnie's shifts closely. The kid had power for sure, but what impressed Bud was his instinct—when to move, when to hold, how to shield the puck.

Arnie won a battle along the boards, spun off a defender, and fired a shot. The goalie smothered it, freezing play.

"That was a good look," Bud murmured.

Sly didn't look up from his book. "Too high on the release. But he's adjusting."

Bud smiled.

But then he felt Gena tense beside him.

Her breathing hitched. Shoulders tightened. Eyes darted up, scanning the crowd again.

"What is it?" Bud asked quietly.

"I—" She took a shaky breath. "I don't know."

Bud kept his voice calm. "Take your time."

She angled away from the ice, clutching her coat. He saw the tremor in her fingers—the same one she tried to hide when clipping her seatbelt or brushing her hair. He knew this version of her. The version that spiraled when the world felt like it was closing in.

But this was public. Loud. Crowded.

She needed gentleness, not caution.

"Let's step out for a minute," Bud whispered. "Fresh air might help."

"No," she said too quickly. "No. Arnie—he'd look up and… I can't leave."

Bud nodded. "Okay. We'll stay."

He slid his hand over hers again. She let him. Her grip tightened enough to hurt.

On the ice, Arnie jumped over the boards for his next shift. The Bears won possession, carrying the puck into the offensive zone. Arnie positioned himself perfectly—low slot, stick on the ice.

A teammate sent him a crisp pass.

Arnie fired.

The puck rocketed past the goalie's glove and into the top corner.

The crowd erupted. Parents stood cheering. Sly even looked up from his book.

"Nice," Sly muttered, hiding a grin behind his hand.

Arnie turned instantly toward the bleachers, scanning for his family.

Bud stood, cheering with the others—loud, unrestrained for once.

But beside him, Gena didn't move. She didn't clap. She didn't smile.

Instead, she froze.

Her face went pale. Her breath stuttered. Her eyes widened as if something massive and invisible had entered the rink.

"Gena?" Bud urged, lowering his voice. "Honey. Talk to me."

She shook her head violently, tears forming too fast.

"I—I can't—Bud, I can't—"

Bud moved in front of her just as she stood abruptly, almost knocking into Sly. Her breaths came fast now, too fast.

"Mom?" Sly said, alarmed.

"I can't be here," she whispered, voice cracking. "I can't—I'm sorry—I have to go—"

And before Bud could say anything, she pushed past him, nearly stumbling down the bleacher steps.

Bud stood frozen for a half second.

Then years of experience told him: Follow her. Now.

"Sly," Bud said sharply. "Stay here. Keep watching your brother. I'll get Mom."

Sly nodded, though worry creased his face.

Bud hurried down the steps after her. By the time he reached the concourse, Gena was near the exit doors, bracing herself against the wall, shoulders shaking.

He slowed his pace intentionally, not wanting to overwhelm her.

"Gena," he whispered, approaching gently. "I'm here."

She flinched as if even his voice hurt.

People glanced over, trying not to stare. Parents with hot chocolates. Kids wobbling on skates. The normal hum of a Saturday rink wrapped around them like insulation—unaware of the storm breaking inside her.

Bud stepped closer, placing a tentative hand on her arm.

"Talk to me," he murmured.

Her voice cracked open. She looked at him with eyes full of fear and shame.

"I just… I saw him score and… everyone cheering and… I felt like I didn't deserve to see it. I felt like I didn't belong. Like I was… ruining everything."

Bud's heart tightened painfully.

"You're not ruining anything," he whispered. "You're their mother."

"I can't be what they need," she said, tears falling. "I can barely be what I need."

Bud shook his head. "Gena—listen to me. You showed up. That's enough. That's more than enough."

She shook her head harder. "It's not. I can't… I can't breathe in there."

"Then breathe out here," he said gently. "We'll take a minute."

"I should go home."

"No," Bud said firmly but softly. "Don't leave. Not yet. Arnie's going to look for you after the period ends. He'll want to see you cheering. Even if it's just once. Even if it's small."

"I can't face everyone after—after this."

"No one's watching us," Bud said. "They're watching their kids. Just like we are."

Gena pressed a hand to her mouth, shaking. "I hate this. I hate this so much."

Bud pulled her into a gentle embrace—not forceful, not tight, just enough for her to feel something steady. She stiffened at first, then slowly, painfully, she let herself lean into him.

"It's okay," he whispered. "Just stay with me. Right here. That's all."

Her breath hitched again, but she didn't pull away.

After a long moment, she whispered, "I miss being normal."

Bud closed his eyes. Quietly, he said:

"You're still you, Gena. Just… tired. Hurt. And healing hurts. I wish I could make it easier. I can't. But I'm here."

She nodded against his chest.

A buzzer sounded for the end of the period.

Bud gently stepped back. "You want to sit out here a bit? We don't have to go back in right away."

Gena wiped her cheeks with the back of her glove. "I'll try. Just… give me a minute."

Bud nodded. "Take all the time you need."

He stayed with her in the concourse, letting the cold air from the open doors wash over them. People passed by, oblivious. Just a husband and wife talking. Just a woman catching her breath.

Nothing dramatic. Nothing unusual. And yet for them, it was everything.

After a few minutes, Gena inhaled deeply and straightened.

"I don't want Arnie to see me like that," she said.

Bud didn't say, "He already did." Instead, he said:

"Then let's go back before he comes looking."

She nodded.

They walked back to the bleachers slowly, hand in hand.

Bud looked at her in profile—tired, shaken, but trying.

Trying still mattered.

When they reached their seats, Sly looked relieved. Arnie was back on the bench, glancing up toward them between shifts.

Gena managed a small wave. Arnie brightened immediately.

And Bud, watching the exchange, felt something tighten and soften inside him at the same time.

He didn't know how long he could keep the pieces together.

But he would try. For them. For her. For today.

Tomorrow could come later.

CHAPTER FOUR
Masks and Meetings

Bud always felt a strange kind of quiet settle over him on the mornings he went into the Augusta office. Not calm. Not dread. Something in between. Like putting on a suit of clothes that didn't quite fit anymore—functional but stiff at the seams.

He parked the truck in the state office lot just before eight, the winter cold biting even through his wool coat. Frost clung to the edges of the windows and the building's concrete steps. The gray sky overhead matched the color of the federal building in the kind of poetic symmetry Bud didn't put much stock in anymore.

He grabbed his thermos, locked the truck, and walked toward the entrance, nodding at a few employees hustling in ahead of him. Most were still juggling coffee cups and messenger bags, stamping their feet against the cold.

Inside, the warmth hit hard—dry, recycled, tinged with the smell of disinfectant. Bud signed in at the small security desk, slid his badge across the scanner, and headed down the corridor toward the elevators. He always took the stairs instead—four flights cleared his head better than being trapped in a metal box.

By the time he reached the third floor, the hallway noise had picked up. Phones rang behind half-closed office doors. Printers hummed, fax machines beeped, and a half-dozen conversations drifted from cubicles like overlapping static.

Bud stepped into his shared office space—a modest room with two desks, a whiteboard filled with budget figures, and a corkboard pinned with maps of local farm plots.

His coworker, Rick Caldwell, was already there, tapping keys furiously while holding a bagel between his teeth. A middle-aged man with thinning hair and a sense of humor that tried too hard, Rick greeted Bud with a muffled, "Murrning."

Bud chuckled. "You choke on that thing; I'm letting you go out dramatically."

Rick swallowed. "Appreciate the support, Day. Real team spirit."

Bud hung his coat and settled at his desk. The computer hummed to life, blue light flickering across his face. He scanned his calendar: weekly grant oversight meeting at nine, field audit scheduling at ten, quote request for fencing subsidies, three voicemails from farmers, and a flagged email from the DC regional division that already felt like a headache waiting to bloom.

"You see the numbers from District 7 yet?" Rick asked, spinning his chair around.

Bud rubbed the bridge of his nose. "Not yet."

"They're bad," Rick said. "Like… someone's-pulling-money-from-beneath-our-noses bad."

Bud's jaw tightened. "Who signed off on them?"

"State liaison's office," Rick said. "But the approvals went through DC without our standard review."

Bud's hands stilled.

He didn't react outwardly, but something deep inside shifted—a subtle awareness, the early steps of danger creeping under the door.

Bud clicked open the message flagged from DC. The email was polite, upbeat, riddled with bureaucratic phrasing that attempted to sound supportive while actually telling him to be quiet.

"Grant cycle adjustments approved," it read. "Further oversight unnecessary at this time." "Please align local expectations with federal direction."

Translation: Stop asking questions and do as you're told.

Bud sat back in his chair, exhaling slowly. It was too early in the day for this kind of dishonesty.

Rick leaned forward. "You okay?"

Bud forced a small smile. "Fine. Just… déjà vu." Then, more quietly: "We'll look into it after the meeting."

Rick nodded, relieved Bud was taking lead. It always settled the rest of them when he did.

At nine o'clock sharp, Bud and Rick entered the conference room. A dozen people were already seated—analysts, field auditors, administrative staff. The usual spread of pastries and coffee cups cluttered the table. The atmosphere hummed with Monday energy: tired, mildly optimistic, edging toward stress.

Susan Talbot, the regional director for Maine, stood at the head of the table. Sharp suit, sharper eyes. A woman who managed both budgets and people with equal efficiency.

"Morning, everyone," she said. "Let's get started."

They reviewed livestock subsidy cycles, fencing grant requests, farm diversification proposals, and storm damage relief efforts. Bud took notes mechanically, his mind both in the room and half a step outside it, where he observed the subtleties others missed—the tremor in Susan's voice mentioning DC involvement, the sideways glances exchanged between two junior staffers, the poorly concealed frustration behind the state veterinarian's tight jaw.

Something was off.

Something had been off for months.

"Bud," Susan said suddenly, pulling him back to the moment. "Your perspective on the Somali Micro-Farm Initiative?"

He sat up straighter.

The room quieted.

The Somali program wasn't massive, but it was politically visible—an initiative designed to support immigrant farming families, offering seed grants and livestock subsidies to help them start small operations. Bud had visited dozens of them. He respected their work ethic. Their pride. Their caution around bureaucracy.

"It's functioning," Bud said. "But we need more oversight on the back end. A few farms are asking for adjustments that don't match field conditions. Nothing criminal. Just… unclear paperwork."

Rick nodded beside him.

Susan tapped her pen. "Unclear how?"

Bud chose his words carefully. "Some of the expansion grants don't align with property size or livestock counts. I think they're overwhelmed with the documentation requirements. We need to send someone out to walk them through it."

A few people exhaled in relief. Bud had a way of diffusing tension without dismissing it.

Susan nodded. "Schedule those visits. And prioritize the Hassan farm—they're up for renewal."

Bud's eyebrows lifted just slightly. "They are?"

"Yes," she said. "Their grant triples next cycle."

Bud masked his reaction.

Triples? Why? Nothing about their operation justified that level of increase. Not unless someone was artificially inflating numbers.

He nodded slowly. "I'll handle it."

"Good," Susan said. "Meeting adjourned."

People gathered their papers, chairs scraping softly. Rick leaned in.

"You feel that?" he whispered.

Bud nodded. "Yeah."

"Something's wrong."

"Something's changing," Bud corrected. "Wrong hasn't been proven yet."

Rick smiled weakly. "That's your optimism talking."

Bud didn't reply.

* * *

Back at his desk, Bud spent an hour reviewing files. Numbers that should have made sense didn't. Reports had been altered. Someone had approved three budgets on the same day with no supporting documentation. And the Hassan family—the quiet, humble folks he'd passed that morning—were suddenly receiving funding levels normally reserved for industrial-scale operations.

It wasn't corruption that bothered him. It was the sloppiness.

Corruption was tidy. It hid itself.

This was rushed. Chaotic. Strange.

At noon, he grabbed a sandwich from the break room and sat alone at the far table, away from chatter. Bud liked background noise—enough to blend into. But he'd never been good at lunch-table politics or office gossip. He preferred silence with his food.

While he ate, he pulled out his phone and scrolled his messages.

Two from Sly—one a question about molecular biomechanics he didn't understand, the other a picture of Arnie in a victory pose after last week's game.

A missed call from Gena.

No voicemail.

He frowned. That wasn't like her.

He wiped his hands and stepped into the hallway, dialing her back.

Three rings. Then—

"Bud?" Her voice sounded thin. Fragile.

"You okay?" he asked, lowering his tone automatically.

"I'm… dizzy," she whispered. "And I… I don't want to interrupt your day."

"You didn't," he said. "Talk to me. What happened?"

"I just… got overwhelmed. I tried to clean the kitchen and suddenly everything felt wrong. Too loud. Too fast. I don't know. I didn't want to bother you."

Bud closed his eyes briefly. His thumb rubbed along the edge of the phone.

"You're never bothering me, Gena. Listen, sit down. Drink some water. I'll stop by the house after work."

"No," she said quickly. "You don't need to come home. I'll be fine. I promise."

He paused, swallowing the frustration that rose uninvited.

"I'll check in again at three," he said gently. "If you're worse, I'm coming home."

"Okay," she whispered.

"Love you," he said softly.

A long silence. Then: "You too."

He ended the call slowly.

The hallway felt colder.

When Bud returned to his desk, Rick looked up. "Everything okay?"

Bud forced a small nod. "Fine."

Rick didn't press. He'd seen that answer before.

An hour later, Bud opened the Hassan file again. The inflated numbers gnawed at him. He highlighted the discrepancies, added notes, and printed out a field-visit schedule.

Tomorrow.

He would visit them tomorrow.

Because someone needed to go. Someone needed to care. And everyone else was either blind or pretending to be.

* * *

At four-thirty, Bud shut down his computer.

He zipped his coat, grabbed his thermos, and stepped into the cold again.

The air outside smelled like coming snow.

He walked toward his truck, boots crunching, breath fogging, the day's weight settling onto his shoulders.

He'd held steady through the meeting. Held steady through the calls.

Held steady through the unease creeping through his professional world.

But none of it compared to the quiet question rising in his chest as he slid into the cab and closed the door.

How long could he stay steady at home?

He didn't have an answer.

He only knew tomorrow he'd step back into the woods—but not for peace.

For the first hint of danger.

And he wasn't sure which version of himself the coming days would demand.

CHAPTER FIVE
Field Lines

Mist clung low over the ground as Bud drove toward the Hassan farm the next morning, turning the dirt road into a pale ribbon winding through frost-tipped fields. The sun hadn't broken fully over the ridgeline yet, leaving the world soft and blue, the way it always looked just before something important happened—good or bad.

Bud tapped the steering wheel with two fingers, a slow, absent rhythm. The truck heater fought the cold, barely winning. The M14 lay secured behind the seat—not because he needed it today, but because he didn't go anywhere rural without it anymore. Old habits died slow, and some habits weren't meant to die at all.

He passed a cluster of bare maples, their branches reaching like thin hands toward the sky. Off to the left, smoke drifted from a lean farmhouse chimney. The Hassan place.

He slowed before he reached the drive.

Something about the quiet felt heavier than usual.

He pulled in, the tires crunching over gravel. Children's bicycles leaned against the porch—one missing a pedal, another missing a handlebar grip.

A soccer ball lay half-buried in the frost near a stump. A small flock of chickens scratched halfheartedly at the frozen ground.

The house itself was worn, patched with care, and alive in a way that spoke of people trying to build something better than what they'd escaped. Bud always admired that. Survival wasn't enough for some families—they wanted progress.

Bud stepped out and shut the door gently. His breath fogged as he adjusted his coat and walked up the porch steps. He knocked once, knuckles echoing faintly.

A second passed. Then another. Then the latch turned.

Hassan opened the door—a tall man with lines of experience etched into his face, dark eyes steady but tired. He wore a fleece jacket over work clothes, boots caked with mud.

"Mr. Day," Hassan said, offering a respectful nod. "Peace be upon you."

"And with you," Bud said, returning the nod. "Sorry for the early hour. Wanted to catch you before chores."

"You catch us during chores," Hassan said, a faint smile touching his lips. "Better timing."

He stepped aside. "Come in. Tea?"

"Only if you're having some," Bud said.

Hassan nodded and gestured toward the small kitchen. The warmth inside the house felt alive—oil heater humming, spices clinging to the air, children's laughter drifting faintly from the back room.

Bud sat at the worn kitchen table while Hassan poured hot tea into a pair of mismatched mugs. The liquid smelled like cinnamon and something floral.

"How's the family?" Bud asked.

"Good," Hassan said. "Tired. Winter is always harder." He handed Bud a mug. "Your sons? Hockey season now?"

Bud nodded. "Arnie scored yesterday."

"Good boy," Hassan said. "Strong legs."

Bud smiled faintly. "Strong everything."

Hassan sat across from him, warming his hands around the mug. "You come for the renewal forms."

"I did," Bud said. "And to walk the fields."

Hassan's expression tightened—not fear exactly, but something uneasy beneath the surface.

"Of course," he said. "We have nothing to hide."

Bud studied him quietly.

Families who had nothing to hide usually said it with confidence. Families who had something to hide said it defensively.

But Hassan said it like a man accustomed to being misunderstood.

Bud reached into his bag and slid the paperwork across the table. "Your numbers jumped this cycle."

"Yes," Hassan said. "We expanded."

"Expanded how?" Bud asked.

Hassan drew in a slow breath. "We were told to. Encouraged, you might say."

Bud sat back. "By who?"

Hassan hesitated. His gaze drifted toward the hallway where his children murmured softly, then back to Bud.

"A man from the district office came. Not from Augusta. From Washington, I think. He said there was new opportunity. New money. That we qualified."

Bud's jaw clenched.

"Did he leave a name?" Bud asked.

"No," Hassan said. "But he had papers. Official papers."

Bud waited.

"He said we must apply for the expansion. That if we did not, we could lose what we already have. It felt like… pressure."

The hairs on Bud's arms stood up.

"Did he mention livestock requirements? Or crop diversification?"

"Both," Hassan said. "But he did not look at our fields. Did not ask what we were capable of. He only said the numbers were decided."

Bud tapped the form with his index finger. "These numbers aren't possible. Not with the size of your land, not with the equipment you have."

Hassan swallowed. "I know."

Silence settled between them—heavy, thick, human.

"You didn't ask for this increase," Bud said quietly.

"No," Hassan said. "But if I refuse… they will think we are ungrateful. Or that we are cheating. We are not cheating. We work hard. But this? It is too much. Too fast."

Bud nodded slowly. "I'll walk the fields."

Hassan stood. "I will go with you."

Bud followed him out the back door into the crisp morning. Frost-laced grass crunched beneath their boots. The fields stretched out behind the house—modest, tended with care, nothing like the industrial-level numbers the paperwork claimed.

Children played near the chicken coop, their laughter bright and clear. The youngest—maybe six—spotted Bud and waved energetically. Bud waved back.

"You saved my family, you know," Hassan said quietly as they walked. "In Somalia. Long ago."

Bud stiffened.

"I didn't know that was you," he said.

"It was not me," Hassan replied. "But it was my brother's family. You carried his son from the alley when fighting broke through the market. You stayed until the Rangers came."

Bud nodded once, swallowing hard. "I remember the boy."

"He remembers you," Hassan said. "He lives in Minnesota now. Strong man. Good father."

Bud breathed slowly, steadying the ache forming behind his ribs.

Hassan continued, "We came here because this land felt quiet. Safe. But lately…" He shook his head. "Something is changing. Men come who do not understand farming. They ask questions that do not belong to agriculture."

Bud studied him. "What kind of questions?"

"About community leaders. About who we respect. Who we listen to. Who we fear." Hassan's voice lowered. "They were not from USDA. I am sure of it."

Bud felt the old instinct rise—the one that told him when danger was not imagined.

"Did you tell anyone?" he asked.

"No," Hassan said. "Who would listen? Immigrants always sound paranoid when speaking of outsiders." He forced a tired smile. "But you listen. So I speak."

Bud nodded.

They walked the field in silence, Bud taking notes, inspecting fences, jotting livestock headcounts, marking inconsistencies—but not the kind that came from dishonesty. The kind that came from someone else filling out forms on their behalf.

When they returned to the porch, Hassan stopped him.

"Mr. Day," he said quietly. "Should I be worried?"

Bud met his eyes.

He debated lying. Debated softening it.

Instead, he said the truth.

"I don't know yet."

Hassan took a long breath and nodded. "Honest answer."

Bud stepped off the porch.

"And Hassan?" he added, pausing.

"Yes?"

"If anyone else comes asking questions… call me first."

Hassan's gaze softened. "I will."

Bud walked back to his truck, boots crunching on gravel. He climbed into the cab, closed the door, and sat there for a moment, the engine off, the world silent.

Something was wrong. Something large. Something reaching fingers into places it didn't belong.

He felt the first ripple of unease—not panic, not fear, but the cold realization that the quiet life he'd built wasn't as insulated as he'd hoped.

He turned the key, the truck rumbling awake.

As he pulled out onto the road, he glanced in the rearview mirror.

Hassan stood on the porch watching him go.

Not fearful. But waiting.

Bud looked forward again.

Tomorrow, he'd file his report. Tomorrow, he'd raise questions.

But today?

Today, he drove home thinking of Gena's pale face at the rink. Her whispered I don't deserve to see it. Her hands trembling. Her breath cracking.

The woods were quiet. The farm was fragile. His family was breaking.

And somewhere—he didn't know how, or where, or when—three worlds were about to collide.

CHAPTER SIX
Pressure Points

It snowed lightly that night, the flakes drifting in slow, lazy spirals outside the cabin windows. The world looked calm from the outside—peaceful even—but inside, the quiet felt strained, like the silence that follows an argument no one quite knows how to finish.

Bud stood at the kitchen counter after dinner, washing dishes under warm water. Gena dried them quietly beside him. They worked in parallel, synchronized by years of habit. But tonight, she moved just a touch slower, her shoulders rounded, her eyes hollow with exhaustion.

The boys were upstairs—Arnie practicing stickhandling in his room even though Bud had asked him twice not to, and Sly reading something far too advanced for a fifteen-year-old. The thumps above them punctuated the silence.

Bud handed Gena a plate. "You sure you're feeling better?"

She nodded, though her eyes stayed on the towel in her hands. "Just tired."

"That wasn't nothing today," Bud said gently.

Gena's shoulders stiffened. "Bud…"

He softened his voice. "It's okay to talk about it."

She swallowed. "I don't want to ruin a good night."

"It's not ruined."

She blinked quickly, as if pushing back tears she didn't want him to see. "I scared them," she whispered. "The boys. You."

"You didn't scare me."

She gave a small, fragile laugh. "You never admit when you're scared."

Bud paused, plate halfway to the drying rack.

He thought about that. Thought about which parts of himself he'd learned to keep quiet. Thought about the years in uniform, the hours in briefings, the dirt under his nails in Mogadishu, the nights where admitting fear would've meant cracking apart.

He set the plate down carefully.

"Maybe I'm not always good at saying it," he said. "But I worry. A lot."

Her lips trembled. "I'm trying, Bud."

"I know."

"It's just…" She wiped her eyes. "Everyone cheering. The noise. The lights. It all hit me at once. And when Arnie scored, instead of feeling proud, I felt like I didn't belong there. Like I was pretending to be something I'm not."

"You're their mom," Bud said softly. "You belonged more than anyone."

She shook her head slowly. "It didn't feel like that."

Bud reached out but stopped short of touching her—close enough she could lean in if she chose. She didn't.

He sighed quietly. "We'll get through this. One game at a time."

Gena gave a thin smile. "One game at a time."

They finished the dishes without speaking.

When they went upstairs, she paused outside the bedroom to tell him, "I'm going to sleep early."

"Okay."

"Wake me if the boys need anything," she said, though it came out weakly.

"I always do."

She stepped into the bedroom and closed the door, not quite shutting it all the way.

Bud stood there for a long moment, the soft glow of the hallway light outlining him. He felt useless in a way he hadn't felt in years. In combat, you had directives. Protocols. Tools. You knew what the enemy looked like, what the threat sounded like, how fast you needed to move.

This? This was a different kind of fight. A fight he wasn't trained for.

He walked down the hall to check on the boys.

Sly was sprawled on his bed, reading a thick paperback about neural engineering. He looked up briefly. "Mom okay?"

"She will be," Bud said, hoping it wasn't a lie.

Sly studied him with too-old eyes. "You sure?"

Bud managed a smile. "You're the genius. What do you think?"

Sly closed the book gently. "I think you're worried."

Bud ruffled his hair. "That obvious?"

"You don't lean against the doorframe when you're relaxed."

Bud blinked. "No kidding?"

Sly nodded. "Also your jaw does that thing."

Bud touched his jaw reflexively. "What thing?"

"The thing where you clench it on the right side."

Bud shook his head, amused and pained all at once. "You notice everything."

"I can't help it," Sly said. "My brain doesn't switch off like other people's."

Bud softened. "Figuring out how your brain works is half of being a teenager."

Sly glanced past him. "Is Mom mad at us?"

"Never," Bud said firmly. "Not for a second."

Sly nodded, but Bud could tell he wasn't fully convinced.

"And Arnie?" Bud asked.

"In his room. Practicing the same shot over and over. He says he needs to do it exactly the way he did when he scored. Something about 'locking in muscle memory.'"

Bud smiled. "Sounds like him."

"You want me to get him to stop?"

"No. Let him burn off whatever he needs to."

Sly hesitated. "Dad?"

Bud leaned in. "Yeah, buddy?"

"Are we all gonna be okay?"

Bud swallowed.

He knelt beside the bed and rested a hand on Sly's knee. "We're a team. Teams have bad days. But we're gonna stick together. I promise you that."

Sly nodded slowly, trusting him more than Bud felt he deserved.

Bud stood. "Get some sleep soon."

"You too," Sly muttered.

He checked on Arnie next. The boy was in front of his mirror, practicing his slapshot motion without a puck, his form surprisingly good for his age. His reflection caught Bud in the doorway.

"Dad!" Arnie said brightly. "Did you see that? Coach said if I get the shot off faster, I could score more."

"I believe it," Bud said. "But not in the house."

Arnie laughed. "Right. Sorry."

Bud stepped inside. "Proud of your play in the game."

Arnie shrugged, though he glowed. "It was just one goal."

"It was a good goal."

Arnie paused mid-swing. "Is Mom okay?"

Bud nodded. "She's just tired."

"From what?"

Bud hesitated. "Life," he said simply. "Life can get heavy sometimes."

Arnie accepted that—kids who trust their parents often do—and resumed working on his form.

Bud closed the door softly behind him.

Back in the hallway, he stood still, grounding himself with a slow breath. Tomorrow would bring new questions. New places to investigate. New cracks in the carefully controlled world he'd built.

* * *

The next morning, the cold came back with bite. Bud left early, not wanting to wake anyone. The sun was still low when he arrived at the USDA office, the building's windows glowing faintly with the first risers of the day.

When he walked in, Rick looked up from his computer. "Hey. You look like hell."

Bud cracked a weak smile. "You're not wrong."

"Everything okay at home?"

Bud hung his coat. "Hockey game was… a lot."

Rick grunted sympathetically. "Kids' sports. One of the many reasons I have cats instead."

Bud chuckled once. "Fair."

Rick leaned forward. "Anything weird at the Hassan place?"

Bud sat down, pulling out his notes. "Weirder than you'd expect."

"Meaning?"

Bud lowered his voice. "Someone from DC—maybe DC—visited them. Told them to expand. Gave them numbers that didn't match their operation."

Rick's face darkened. "That's not just weird. That's illegal."

"It's something," Bud said. "But we don't know what yet."

Rick shifted in his chair. "Bud… be careful with this."

Bud raised a brow. "You sound like my CO back in the day."

"Well, your CO wasn't wrong," Rick muttered. "Look—when DC starts pushing numbers from the top down? That's never innocent."

Bud's jaw tightened. "I'm not dropping it."

"I figured you'd say that." Rick sighed. "Let me know how deep this goes."

Bud nodded once—an unspoken pact between them.

* * *

By mid-morning, Bud was knee-deep in spreadsheets, numbers, and field maps. The discrepancies weren't limited to the Hassan farm. Four Somali-run farms showed similar inflation. A fifth had two sets of financials logged under the same ID number. And three more had been approved for equipment subsidies they never requested.

Someone was moving money through these operations.

Someone wanted them bloated on paper.

Bud's stomach tightened.

He rubbed his eyes, then noticed a sticky note on his monitor.

CALL FROM LANGLEY — URGENT Extension: 2447

He stared at it for a long moment.

Langley. Not that Langley. A USDA oversight office in Virginia.

Still, the name alone stirred old instincts.

Bud dialed the number.

"Langley Oversight Division, this is Donna."

"This is Senior Analyst Bud Day, calling from the Maine regional office."

"Oh!" she said brightly, though the tone was off. Nervous. "Yes, thank you for calling back. We… had a question regarding your Somali micro-farm audit."

Bud sat straighter. "Go ahead."

"You submitted an internal request this morning for clarification on three funding cycles."

"Yes."

"Well… we would prefer those inquiries go through DC first."

Bud's jaw flexed. "Why is that?"

"We're undergoing a realignment. Certain files are being reorganized. It's all routine."

Routine. Government-speak for stop digging.

Bud kept his voice even. "With respect, ma'am, some of these numbers don't line up. I need to see the original approvals."

"That won't be necessary," she said quickly. "We've confirmed everything is accurate."

"No, you've confirmed everything is filed," Bud corrected.

Silence.

Very faint. Very tense.

"Mr. Day," she said finally, "we appreciate your diligence. But we kindly ask you to focus on new applications for now."

"Noted," Bud said. "But I'll still need the originals."

"We'll… circle back."

Click.

Bud set the phone down slowly.

Something was wrong. Something deep. Something coordinated.

And someone—somewhere—didn't want him looking too closely.

Bud leaned back in his chair and exhaled. The room felt colder than it had a moment ago.

His life had always been split into two worlds: the one he could control, and the one he survived through instinct.

Today, those worlds took a small step toward each other.

He felt the ground shift.

Very slightly. But unmistakably.

CHAPTER SEVEN
Down to the District

Bud hated flying out of Portland in winter. Fog clung to the runways like bad memories, and the cold made the aluminum joints of the jetways creak like old bones. Still, he preferred the early-morning flights—the ones where the airport was quiet, the world hadn't woken yet, and the only voices belonged to tired business travelers and airline staff trying too hard to sound cheerful.

He parked the F-150 in long-term parking, the metal groaning as he shut the door. The air had a bite that cut straight to the ribs. Bud pulled his duffel from the backseat, slung it over his shoulder, and walked toward the terminal.

Inside, the warmth hit him with a wave of conflicting emotions. Airports always triggered something in him—not PTSD, not dread, just… the sense of transition. The sense of stepping between two lives.

Home and everything heavy about it. DC and everything numb about it.

The line for security moved quickly. Travelers shifted from foot to foot, tablets and laptops in hand, patience thinning with every shuffle forward. Bud joined them without complaint. He emptied his pockets with practiced simplicity, placed his boots and belt in the bin, and lifted his duffel onto the conveyor.

The TSA agent looked at him twice—not suspicious, just curious. Older men with military posture tended to earn second glances.

"Morning, sir," the agent said.

Bud gave a nod. "Morning."

"Traveling for business?"

"Unfortunately."

The agent chuckled. "Don't we all."

Bud passed through without issue.

At the gate, he sat near the window, watching ground crew move with brisk efficiency. Yellow vests flashing, wands signaling, trucks rumbling. Everything ordered. Predictable. A far cry from the chaos of grant cycles back in the office—or the chaos inside his own home.

He checked his phone.

A text from Sly: Have a good flight. Bring back donuts. Not from the airport—they taste like sadness.

Bud chuckled.

Then a second text from Arnie: GET A WINDOW SEAT AND LOOK FOR UFOs followed by a dozen alien emojis.

And nothing from Gena.

He didn't know whether to be relieved or worried.

Boarding was calm. Business travelers in wrinkle-free suits. A few tired college students returning from break. Families bundled in winter coats. Bud slipped into his aisle seat, stowed his bag, and settled in as the engines hummed to life.

As the plane rose into the gray morning sky, he stared out at the clouds, their edges tinged with faint pink from a sun that wasn't trying very hard today.

He let the altitude wash his mind clean for a moment.

Maine always felt heavy—emotionally, mentally, spiritually. DC never felt heavy. It just felt empty. And sometimes, empty was easier to manage.

By the time the plane touched down at Reagan National, Bud had shifted into work-mode. His breathing steadied. His spine straightened. The mask slid into place.

* * *

D.C. Always Had a Smell

The airport smelled like disinfectant, roasted coffee, and too many people pretending to be important. Bud grabbed his duffel and headed toward the exit, the familiar buzz of politics and ambition thick in the air.

He caught the Yellow Line into the city, the train humming through tunnels plastered with ads for law schools, defense contractors, and tech start-ups claiming they would save the world.

Outside at L'Enfant Plaza, the wind cut through his coat. The city was cold but not the good kind of cold—not the crisp, cleansing kind of Maine. DC cold was sharp and impatient, pushing people faster than they wanted to move.

He walked the five blocks to the USDA satellite office housed in a squat, forgettable brick building. Federal architecture that somehow managed to look both temporary and permanent.

Inside, the elevator dinged softly, and he rode to the fourth floor. The hallway lights flickered once—maintenance issue, not symbolism. Still, it felt symbolic.

Bud stepped into a narrow office suite filled with cubicles and the smell of burnt coffee. People in suits nodded politely. No one asked how his flight was. No one cared. That was one thing Bud liked about DC: the predictability of apathy.

At the end of the hall, Deputy Director Evan Briggs sat in his office, leaning over a stack of papers. Briggs was the kind of bureaucrat who looked like he'd been born wearing a government badge—clean haircut, clean posture, clean conscience. Or so he claimed.

"Bud," Briggs said, standing to shake his hand. "Glad you could make it on short notice."

"You said it was important."

Briggs gestured for him to sit. "It is. We've had increased attention on the micro-farm program. Congressional interest. Funding expansions. We need everything tidy."

"Tidy," Bud repeated. "That why someone from DC visited my farmers without paperwork?"

Briggs's smile tightened. "Let's not jump to assumptions."

Bud kept his eyes steady. "I don't like people telling my farmers what to apply for."

"They're not your farmers," Briggs said gently. "They're federal grantees."

"They're human beings trying to survive," Bud said. "Somebody's feeding them numbers they can't support. That's not oversight. That's coercion."

Briggs sighed and rubbed his temple. "Look. Things are moving fast. There are pressures from above. Initiatives tied to foreign aid optics, political partnerships, diaspora relations—far above our pay grade."

Bud leaned back. "So we ignore inconsistencies?"

"We prioritize what matters," Briggs said. "And what matters is keeping this program stable through the next funding cycle."

"And if stability is built on lies?"

Briggs shifted, uncomfortable now. "Bud… tread carefully. Please."

That word—carefully—hit Bud in a way he didn't like.

As if Briggs wasn't warning him about paperwork. As if he was warning him about people.

"Noted," Bud said.

Briggs let out a relieved breath and changed the subject. "Your check-in with the oversight liaison is at three. They've assigned someone new for your meeting."

"Who?"

"Special Consultant Westbrook."

Bud frowned. "Don't know the name."

"You will," Briggs said with a small, vague smile.

* * *

The Meeting Before the Meeting

Bud grabbed a coffee from the breakroom and stood by the window overlooking the street. Cars crawled by in sluggish midday traffic. Vendors set up carts. Joggers dodged commuters. A city pretending not to be chaotic.

He checked his phone.

A message from Gena: Made it through the morning. Trying to rest. Love you.

He typed a response, erased it, typed again.

Proud of you. Call me later if you want.

He hit send and pocketed the phone.

Behind him, the breakroom door opened. He expected Rick's DC counterpart or an analyst he vaguely recognized.

Instead, it was a woman he'd never seen.

Late twenties maybe, though her eyes looked older. Dark hair pinned neatly. A clean, tailored jacket. She moved with quiet precision, the kind military or field-trained people had when they tried not to look military or field-trained.

She stepped to the counter, poured coffee, and glanced at him once—polite, brief, but observant.

"Morning," she said softly.

"Morning," Bud replied.

She stirred her coffee slowly. "You're Day, correct? From the Maine office?"

Bud stiffened just slightly. "Yes."

She nodded. "I work on some policy reviews tied to your region. Layla Haddad."

She extended her hand.

Bud shook it, noting the firmness of her grip—not aggressive, just confident.

"Nice to meet you," he said.

"You too," she replied. "I've read your reports."

He raised a brow. "Hope they were clear enough."

"They were," she said. "Clear is rare."

Bud studied her. Something about her tone—calm, measured—felt unusual for DC staff. Most were frantic or performative. She was neither.

Layla glanced at the folder in his hand. "Heading to your oversight briefing?"

"In a bit," Bud said.

She nodded slowly. "Be honest, but be cautious."

Bud blinked. "That supposed to be advice?"

She smiled faintly. "A suggestion."

Then, without another word, she set down her spoon and walked out.

Bud watched her go, a faint knot tightening in his chest.

He didn't know who she was yet. He didn't know how she fit into all this.

He didn't know whether she was ally, obstacle, or something in between.

But his instincts, tuned over decades, whispered the same thing—

Remember her.

* * *

The Oversight Briefing

At three o'clock, Bud entered a small, windowless conference room. Two people sat inside: a senior liaison with a forced smile and a younger man who looked like he'd been pulled from law school orientation.

Bud introduced himself and sat.

The liaison slid a folder toward him. "We received your audit request on the Somali micro-farms. We want to clarify expectations."

Bud folded his hands. "Go ahead."

"We don't want field analysts over-escalating issues that aren't issues yet," the liaison said.

Bud kept his jaw from flexing.

"I'm not escalating," he said. "I'm documenting."

The younger man cleared his throat nervously. "Sir, with the new political pressure on immigration support programs, we need to avoid… negative optics."

"Negative optics," Bud repeated. "Meaning fraud."

"No one said that," the liaison snapped quickly. "We're saying be… selective."

Bud stared at them both.

"So you're asking me not to do my job."

"We're asking you to align with priorities."

Bud glanced at the folder in front of him. Then at the two faces across the table. Then at the door Layla had walked through twenty minutes earlier.

He exhaled slowly. "I'll review my notes and follow up."

They looked relieved.

Bud felt sick.

* * *

Outside the Building

When the meeting ended, he walked outside into the cold, the wind slicing along the sidewalk. He stood near the corner of the block, hands in his coat pockets, staring at the city moving around him.

A familiar emptiness settled in his chest.

DC was where he came to bury things. Maine was where he came to feel them.

And both worlds were starting to bleed into each other.

Bud inhaled the icy air, held it, and exhaled slowly.

Tomorrow, he'd attend the regional policy summit. Tomorrow, he'd meet more people who smiled too easily. Tomorrow, he'd gather information in ways he hadn't used since Kosovo and Somalia.

But tonight?

Tonight, he needed somewhere to think. Somewhere quiet. Somewhere private.

Somewhere like the The Dupont club.

He didn't text or call ahead. He didn't need to. They always knew when he was in town.

As he crossed the street, slipping into the flow of evening commuters, he didn't notice the man sitting in the black SUV across the block.

But the man noticed him.

And made a quiet note.

CHAPTER EIGHT

The Dupont Quiet

Bud walked from the Orange Line to the club instead of transferring to the Red Line at Metro Center. The Metro bothered him enough without the added density. He also wanted the cold. Needed it, even. The winter wind that knifed through his coat cleared his head more than anything he'd heard in the oversight briefing.

DC felt different at night. Less polished. More honest. The marble monuments glowed from a distance like altars. Traffic hummed along Dupont Circle in a steady, restless rhythm. Restaurants filled with diplomats pretending to relax. Young professionals spilled from bars in clusters—too loud, too drunk, too eager to forget the day.

Bud moved through all of it without touching it—just one more ghost in a city built on them.

When he reached the narrow brownstone with the unmarked door, he paused. The streetlamp overhead flickered slightly, washing the entrance in a soft halo. No sign. No address. Just a place you only knew existed if you were meant to.

A single brass knocker shaped like a lion's head gleamed under the lamp. Bud lifted it once.

Knock. Wait.

The door opened smoothly without sound.

"Good evening, Mr. Day," the attendant said—a poised woman in a dark suit. "Welcome back."

Bud nodded. "Evening."

She stepped aside. "Your room is ready."

He entered, the familiar warmth enveloping him immediately. Not heat—the warmth of muted lighting, hushed conversations, soft music drifting from somewhere he could never quite locate.

The Dupont club wasn't a brothel. Not even close. It was a sanctuary, a refuge for people who lived under pressure thick enough to choke on. Politicians, executives, operatives, analysts—people who wore masks for a living. People who needed to take them off somewhere.

Privacy was the currency here. Not bodies. Not secrets. Just permission to exist without performing.

Bud followed the attendant down a hallway adorned with abstract paintings and warm mahogany paneling. He passed two small sitting rooms where soft laughter floated over clinking glasses. A pianist played something quiet in the parlor—jazz, slow and clean.

His room—Room Five—was on the second floor.

The attendant opened the door for him. "She'll be here shortly."

Bud nodded, though something in him tightened at the phrasing. Not discomfort. Not anticipation. Just… the awareness that this was part of the ritual now.

When the attendant left, Bud stepped inside.

The room looked like the lobby of a boutique hotel: soft amber lamp light, a chaise near the window, shelves of books curated for distraction, and a small table set with tea and water. The air smelled faintly of sandalwood.

He hung his coat on the hook by the door and sat.

He didn't come here for what the place offered in the shadows. Not anymore. That had faded slowly over the last year, replaced by something much harder to name. Something closer to needing a witness. Someone who could see him without flinching. Someone who didn't crumble like Gena or walk on eggshells around him like his colleagues.

Someone who didn't expect him to fix anything.

Someone like Layla.

He shook the thought away—not because it was inappropriate, but because it was too early to interrogate. Too soon after meeting her. Too soon after noticing how easily she had seen past the bureaucratic fog surrounding him.

He exhaled slowly.

A soft knock sounded on the door.

"Come in," Bud said.

The door opened, and Layla stepped inside.

For a moment, the room felt smaller.

Not because she looked different—she still wore that calm, poised presence, her hair pulled back loosely, a simple, elegant blouse under a charcoal blazer—but because she looked like she had expected to see him.

"Mr. Day," she said gently. "I hope you don't mind. They said you requested someone for conversation."

Bud blinked once. Slowly. "I didn't request anyone by name."

Her eyes softened. "Then maybe they guessed right."

She closed the door behind her.

Bud stood. "How did you—?"

She smiled faintly. "I consult here sometimes. This is one of the few places where staff from federal agencies can breathe. When your name appeared on tonight's list, they asked if I wanted to cover your slot."

That explained the attendant's tone. It did not explain why Layla had said yes.

Bud cleared his throat, unsure how to proceed. "If this is inappropriate"

"It isn't," she said softly. "Unless you want it to be."

He held her eyes for a beat too long. Then he looked away.

Layla crossed the room and sat on the chaise with effortless composure. "Please. Sit. You look like you've carried a city on your shoulders since sunrise."

Bud hesitated, then sank into the chair facing her.

For a moment, neither spoke.

Layla studied him in that quiet, attentive way of hers. Not evaluating. Not prying. Simply reading—like she was fluent in a language he'd stopped speaking years ago.

"You had a difficult day," she said.

It wasn't a question.

Bud exhaled. "You have no idea."

"Try me."

He considered his words. "Oversight is… shifting. Someone's pushing numbers they shouldn't. Pressuring farmers. Telling me to ignore red flags."

Layla nodded slowly. "Yes."

Bud stilled. "You know."

"I know pieces," she corrected. "Enough to recognize when someone in your position starts attracting attention."

"Attention?" Bud echoed.

"Your report-writing," Layla said. "Your field notes. Your refusal to soften language when the truth is uncomfortable. Those traits are admirable… and dangerous."

Something cold moved through Bud's chest.

"Dangerous to who?" he asked carefully.

"To people who benefit from confusion," she said.

Bud leaned back. "You're speaking in riddles."

"I'm speaking in warnings," Layla corrected. "Quiet ones."

He studied her, slower this time. The club lighting painted her profile in warm gold, emphasizing the calm certainty in her posture. She wasn't afraid. She wasn't reckless. She was simply… aligned with something he didn't yet understand.

"I'm not trying to cause trouble," Bud said.

"I know," she replied. "That's what makes you dangerous. The people causing trouble are never worried about it. The people who worry about it are always the ones standing in their way."

Bud didn't know whether to laugh or curse. "You think I've stepped into something bigger than grants and paperwork?"

"I think," she said, choosing her words carefully, "that you've stepped into a place where money, influence, and political protection blur together. Where your honesty becomes an obstacle."

He rubbed his jaw. "That's not why I do the job."

"Exactly," she whispered.

Silence stretched between them. Comfortable. Heavy. Understanding.

Layla leaned forward slightly. "Tell me something, Bud… do you ever rest?"

He scowled, but only lightly. "I sleep."

"I said rest."

He didn't answer.

She tilted her head, studying him. "You spend your days holding the world up for everyone else. Your wife. Your boys. Your farmers. Your coworkers. Your superiors. Who holds you up?"

No one, Bud almost said.

The woods, maybe. The quiet. The rifle stock against his shoulder.

But no person.

She saw the answer without him giving it.

"That's why you come here," she said softly.

Bud swallowed. "Here's quiet."

"Quiet is not the same as peace," she said gently. "You don't come here for quiet. You come here so you don't break somewhere that would make your family afraid."

The words landed in him like a truth he didn't want to accept.

Layla shifted, her voice warm but firm. "Let me ask again. Do you rest?"

Bud closed his eyes for a moment, letting the room's warmth hold him.

Finally, he said, "I don't know how anymore."

She breathed in slowly. "Then let's start there."

Her words weren't seductive. They weren't flirtatious. They weren't clinical.

They were human.

Something Bud hadn't been offered—honestly, gently—in a very long time.

For the next hour, they talked. Not about secrets. Not about politics. Not about Somalia or Kosovo or anything sharp enough to cut open old wounds.

They talked about sons. About winter in Maine. About the cost of wanting to fix what refuses to be fixed.

At one point, Layla said something that made Bud laugh—really laugh—and she smiled at the sound as if she hadn't heard him do it before.

When the clock on the small table neared ten, Layla rose.

"I should go," she said.

Bud stood with her. "Will I see you again?"

She held his gaze. "You'll see me when you need to."

He opened his mouth to speak, but she stepped closer—just enough that he felt her warmth.

"Not everything has to break, Bud," she whispered. "Some things just need someone who sees them."

And then, with a final, soft nod, she slipped out of the room.

Bud stood in the quiet, feeling something inside him shift—something he hadn't allowed to move in years.

Not desire. Not guilt. Not betrayal.

Recognition.

Of himself. Of her. Of the fact that something was changing.

Something was already in motion.

He left the club an hour later, stepping into the cold DC night.

Someone in a parked SUV across the street watched him leave.

Bud didn't see them.

But they saw him.

CHAPTER NINE
Signals

The city looked different in the morning after a night at the Dupont club. Not cleaner. Not brighter. Just more… exposed.

Bud stepped out of his hotel onto a narrow K Street sidewalk, coffee in hand, coat collar turned up against the wind. The sky was the color of old asphalt—no promise of sun, just a flat gray that matched the mood in most federal buildings this time of year.

He'd slept, technically. Four hours. Enough to keep his mind sharp, not enough to take the weight off his shoulders. Conversation with Layla lingered in his thoughts—not the words so much as the way she'd looked at him like he was still a man worth listening to.

He pushed that thought aside.

Today wasn't about feelings. Today was about signals.

The policy summit was in one of those DC hotels that all looked the same—over-air-conditioned, over-carpeted, over-priced. Bud slipped through the revolving door into a lobby full of people wearing name badges and performing importance.

Banners hung along the walls:

AGRICULTURAL FUTURES & COMMUNITY RESILIENCE SUMMIT

Underneath, in smaller print:

Sponsored by: USDA, Select NGOs, Strategic Partners

"Strategic partners," Bud thought. Always such a polite way to say, "the people with money."

He checked in at the registration desk, received a lanyard with his name on it, and walked toward the main conference room. The air buzzed with conversations about carbon credits, regenerative soil, data analytics, and "optimizing outputs." Not a lot of talk about families. Or trust.

Inside, rows of round tables faced a stage where a large screen cycled through sponsor logos. Bud picked a table near the middle—close enough to see, far enough not to be noticed.

He scanned the room instinctively.

Briggs sat near the front with a cluster of DC staffers. A few faces Bud recognized from Teams meetings but had never met in person. Two men in suits that were slightly too nice to be federal salaries sat alone at a side table, their badges flipped backward.

Lobbyists, he guessed. Or worse.

On the far side of the room, he spotted Layla, standing near a coffee station, speaking quietly with an older woman in a navy blazer. Layla held a folder against her chest, posture relaxed but purposeful.

Even from here, Bud could tell she'd shifted into a different mode. Not the quiet sanctuary of the club. Not the casual warmth of the breakroom. This was her professional skin: calm, direct, ready.

She glanced up briefly, scanning the room.

Her eyes found his.

For a heartbeat, the noise of the summit faded.

She gave the slightest nod—acknowledgment, not invitation.

He returned it.

Then the moment passed, and the crowd swallowed them both again.

* * *

The opening keynote was the usual blend of buzzwords and cautious optimism. A Deputy Undersecretary with a perfectly polished speech talked about "leveraging agricultural opportunity" and "empowering vulnerable communities." Applause came at the right places. People took notes they would never read again.

Bud listened with half an ear and two-thirds suspicion.

When the session broke into smaller panels, he attended the one that mattered: "Grant Oversight & Community Trust: Best Practices in Immigrant Farming Support."

He almost laughed at the title.

Inside the breakout room, chairs were set in a loose semi-circle. A panel of five sat at the front: two policy analysts, one NGO representative, a lawyer from some advocacy group, and—Bud's stomach tightened when he saw her—Layla.

She sat at the far right end of the table, legal pad in front of her, pen aligned perfectly along the margin.

The moderator welcomed everyone, then gestured to each panelist with practiced enthusiasm.

Layla was introduced last.

"Ms. Layla Haddad, Special Consultant on Agricultural Policy and Legal Compliance, with a focus on grant integrity and vulnerable communities."

Bud raised an eyebrow. Grant integrity.

Interesting.

The first twenty minutes were standard panel fare. Questions about balancing oversight with cultural sensitivity. Concerns over documentation burdens. Strategies for avoiding predatory lending. Nothing he hadn't heard before, nothing that hinted at the rot he'd smelled in the Somali micro-farm program.

Then someone in the audience asked the question he'd been waiting for.

"What do we do," a woman from a Midwest NGO asked, "when we suspect political pressure is shaping grant allocation in ways that don't match what's happening on the ground?"

The room shifted. People stopped typing. Stopped stirring their coffee.

The first two panelists answered with diplomatic non-answers—oversight frameworks, audit processes, internal review mechanisms. All the usual phrases that sounded reassuring without meaning anything.

Then the moderator turned to Layla.

"Ms. Haddad, your thoughts?"

Layla paused, pen resting lightly in her fingers.

"When oversight becomes political," she said slowly, "we have to ask a different question."

The moderator blinked. "Which is?"

"Is the purpose of the program to help people," she said, "or to help numbers look like we helped people?"

A quiet murmur rippled through the room.

"Sometimes," Layla continued calmly, "we see funding patterns that don't make sense based on farm capacity, land size, or local conditions. That can happen for benign reasons—poor training, rushed paperwork. But it can also happen when outside interests are involved: contractors, foreign influencers, domestic political actors."

Someone coughed sharply in the back.

"If analysts in the field are raising consistent concerns," Layla said, "and those concerns are systematically minimized, redirected, or discouraged, that's a signal. Not proof. Not yet. But a signal worth respecting."

The moderator cleared his throat nervously. "And what would you advise field analysts do under those conditions?"

"Two things," Layla said. "Document everything. And find allies who value integrity more than stability."

Her eyes flickered, just once, toward Bud.

He didn't move. Didn't break eye contact. Didn't look away.

He felt the temperature in the room change, just slightly. Not for everyone. Just for the few who knew exactly what she was really saying.

He wondered how many that was.

* * *

After the panel, people crowded the front to ask follow-up questions. Bud waited until the line thinned, then approached the table.

Layla was collecting her notes, sliding them into a folder with practiced neatness.

"Good panel," Bud said.

She glanced up, the corner of her mouth tilting. "You mean mildly subversive for a government conference?"

"Something like that."

She closed the folder. "You looked unimpressed during the keynote."

"I was impressed," he said. "Just not with the speaking."

She smiled more fully at that.

"Walk with me?" she asked.

They stepped out into the hallway, letting the crowd move past them toward the next round of sessions. The noise muffled around them like static.

"Anything new from Maine?" she asked.

Bud nodded. "More farms. Same pattern. Hassan family confirmed someone from DC pressured them into higher-level funding."

She exhaled slowly through her nose. "That tracks with what I'm seeing from this side."

"What are you seeing?"

"Unusual clustering in one demographic subgroup," Layla said. "Funding expansions tied to districts with certain political donors. High-volume approvals stamped by the same handful of people."

"That all?" Bud asked dryly.

"That's all I can prove," she said. "For now."

They reached a quiet alcove near a side exit. A large potted plant did a poor job of pretending they had privacy.

"You need to be careful," Layla said softly. "They've flagged your file."

Bud's shoulders tightened. "Who's 'they'?"

"The people who like stable numbers and quiet reports," she replied. "The people who think oversight is a threat to their revenue streams. The people who don't like that you keep asking for original approvals."

"A lot of people," Bud said.

"Exactly," she murmured.

Bud watched her closely. "Where do you sit in all this, Layla?"

"Between," she said simply.

He frowned. "That sounds like a dangerous place to stand."

"It is," she admitted. "But it's where I can see the most."

He believed her. That was what unsettled him.

"You talk like somebody who's worn a uniform," he said quietly.

She tilted her head. "I haven't. But my father did. Army. Military police. I grew up around men who thought the regs were scripture and the chain of command was sacred."

"How'd they feel about you going into law and policy?"

"They thought it was safer," she said. A small, humorless smile. "Turns out, they were wrong."

Silence settled between them for a moment.

"You're going back to Maine tomorrow?" she asked.

"Yeah."

"Check on Hassan again," she said. "And if you see anyone new around their property—anyone they introduce as 'friends of the program'—you call me."

He nodded. "How far does this go, Layla?"

She held his gaze. "Farther than either of us wants to admit."

"And Somalia?" he asked quietly.

The name hung between them like a third presence.

Her eyes flickered. "What about it?"

"I don't believe in coincidences."

"I don't either," she said. "And no, it's not a coincidence that Somali-backed NGOs are showing up in your state's funding streams. Or that certain foreign donors are suddenly interested in American micro-farms."

"Foreign donors like who?"

She shook her head. "Names later. Right now, you need to focus on patterns, not villains."

"Patterns still come with bodies in my experience," Bud said.

She studied him. "Spoken like someone who's seen both."

He exhaled. "Too many."

A notification buzzed on her phone. She glanced at it, then back at him.

"I have to brief someone upstairs," she said. "Not one of the bad ones, for once."

"Good," Bud said.

"You going back to your hotel?"

"Later."

"Be careful where 'later' is," she said softly. "The club isn't as invisible as it thinks it is."

He went still.

"Meaning?" he asked.

"Meaning," she replied carefully, "the more you mix personal refuge with political pressure, the more likely someone is to exploit that."

He stared at her. "Is that a warning?"

"Consider it a courtesy," she said. "I like straightforward men who still believe in doing their jobs right. I'd prefer you not end up in someone's file as leverage."

Bud swallowed.

"Thanks," he said.

Layla nodded once, then turned and walked back toward the conference, disappearing into the current of suits and badges.

Bud stood there a moment longer, feeling the threads around him tighten. He checked his watch. He had an hour before his next session. He didn't want to sit through another panel on "optimization" or "stakeholder synergy." He needed air. Movement. Checkpoints.

Outside the hotel, the cold hit him again, sharper now. He walked a full block before he realized he was taking stock of his surroundings the way he did downrange: street exits, vehicles with idling engines, sight lines from rooftops.

He noticed a dark sedan parked across from the hotel entrance.

Same one from last night?

Hard to say. Could've been any one of a hundred sedans in this city. But his instincts didn't care about probability. They cared about patterns.

The driver pretended to look at his phone, but his eyes kept lifting—scanning the foot traffic, lingering a half-second too long whenever anyone with a government badge walked past.

Bud slowed, adjusted his path, and circled the block.

By the time he came around again, the car was gone.

Coincidence? Maybe.

He didn't believe in them. Not anymore.

His phone vibrated in his pocket.

A text from Gena: Made it to Arnie's practice. Stayed the whole time. No meltdown. Small victory.

Another from Sly: Mom did good. Donuts still pending.

Bud smiled despite the tension coiling tighter around his spine.

He typed back: Tell Mom I'm proud of her. And of you both. Donuts incoming when I'm home.

He put the phone away, looked back once more at the hotel, and exhaled.

The world had layers now. Farmers, numbers, DC, clubs, cars that might be nothing. A woman who saw too much. A wife hanging on by raw fingertips.

And beneath it all, the quiet, patient feeling he recognized from other parts of his life—

The sense that something big was coming.

He had no way of knowing, standing there in the DC cold with his hands in his pockets and worry in his chest, that the next time he drove up the Hassan road, nothing about their quiet farm would feel safe again.

For now, all he knew was this:

He was in something. Deeper than he'd planned. And turning back was already off the table.

CHAPTER TEN

The Edge of the Map

The flight back to Portland was bumpy, the kind of turbulence that rattled overhead bins and made passengers grip armrests a little tighter than they wanted to admit. Bud didn't mind. He'd flown through worse—weather and otherwise. Still, each jolt tugged him out of the maze of thoughts he'd been walking since leaving DC.

Layla's warning replayed in his head in pieces, like fragments of a radio signal:

…your file has been flagged. …integrity is dangerous to certain people.

…the club isn't as private as you think. …find allies who value truth over stability.

He'd spent the entire flight trying to determine which part bothered him the most. Turned out, it was all of them.

By the time the wheels hit the runway in Portland, Bud's jaw ached from clenching. He switched his phone off airplane mode and waited for the signal to catch.

Three texts came through from Gena.

1:10 PM — Can you pick up milk on your way home? 3:46 PM — Boys arguing over gloves again. Normal chaos. 5:02 PM — You landing soon?

He exhaled softly.

No meltdowns. No frantic messages. No emotional collapses.

A good day by their new standard.

He texted back: Just landed. Milk, yes. See you soon.

Before retrieving his luggage, he stopped in the restroom to splash cold water on his face. The mirror reflected someone who hadn't truly rested in far too long. A man who was trying to balance two worlds that no longer fit together comfortably.

He dried his face, grabbed his duffel, and headed toward the exit.

Outside, the wind was sharper than when he'd left—northbound, biting. The kind of cold that worked its way into bones and stayed there.

On the drive home, Portland thinned into pine forests, then rural roads, then the quiet that Bud used to think of as peace. Now it felt like an unresolved question.

By the time the cabin came into view—chimney smoking, porch light on, snow piled at the corners of the drive—twilight had settled into a blue-gray hush

Moose barked from inside the cabin as Bud pulled up. The dog's tail thumped against the door before Bud even set foot inside.

"Hey, Moose," he murmured, rubbing the dog's head. "Miss me, huh?"

The boys were at the kitchen table—Arnie poking a mashed potato mountain with a fork, Sly reading something on his tablet while pretending not to watch the door.

Gena stood at the stove stirring a pot of stew.

She turned as Bud walked in.

Her smile was small but real. "Welcome home."

The warmth of those words surprised him more than he cared to admit.

"Good to be home," he said.

He crossed the kitchen, kissed her cheek lightly, and set the milk on the counter.

"You eat yet?" she asked.

"On the plane," he lied. The pretzel pack hadn't counted, but he didn't want her worrying about whether he was hungry.

Arnie launched into a story before Bud could sit.

"Dad! Coach said if I keep practicing my release angle, I might get moved up a line!"

Bud grinned. "Nice. You've been working hard."

Sly added quietly, "He's also been working loud. I can verify."

Arnie jabbed him with his elbow. "Hey!"

Sly smirked, not looking up from his tablet.

The exchange might've devolved into bickering, but Gena intervened with a soft clap of her hands.

"Alright, give your father a minute to breathe."

They actually obeyed.

Bud took his seat at the table. For a few minutes, it was almost normal—laughing, eating, telling small stories. A kind of domestic truce.

He caught Gena's eyes once and saw something softer there. Not healed, not whole, but grateful.

He wished he felt worthy of that gratitude.

* * *

After dinner, the boys retreated upstairs. Moose followed them halfway before deciding Bud's side was the better destination.

Gena washed dishes while Bud dried. A rhythm as familiar as their marriage, though the pauses between movements felt heavier these days.

"How was DC?" she asked finally.

Bud hesitated.

He wanted to tell her the truth—that someone might be watching him, that Layla Haddad had given him a warning wrapped in a conversation, that pressures he didn't yet understand were closing in.

But he didn't want to add weight to shoulders already collapsing under their own burdens.

"It was fine," he said.

Gena studied him quietly. "You look tired."

"So do you," he said gently.

She gave him a small, sad smile. "I try."

He wanted to reach for her. Not romantically. Just to offer something warm. But connection had become a complicated equation—for both of them.

Instead, he handed her the last plate.

"I'm going to step outside for a bit," he said.

"Okay."

He pulled on his coat and stepped onto the back porch. The cold hit him immediately, crystallizing on his eyelashes, turning his breath into fog. The woods behind the cabin were still, a dark silhouette against the fading light.

Bud stood on the porch for a long time, breathing the cold, letting it ground him.

Something was wrong.

He didn't know where the first domino was. But he could feel the table vibrating.

He didn't hear Gena come up behind him until she spoke.

"You're thinking loudly."

He turned slightly. "Sorry."

"You don't have to apologize," she said softly.

He faced her fully.

Her eyes were clearer than he expected. "Bud… I know I'm not the easiest person to live with right now."

"You're not supposed to be easy," he said. "You're supposed to be you. Whatever that looks like."

She looked away, her breath forming a thin cloud. "I wish I could explain what's happening in my head. Sometimes it feels like I'm drowning in a shallow pool—like if I just stood up, I'd be fine, but I can't make my legs move."

Bud swallowed hard. "I'm not going anywhere."

She nodded, tears glistening lightly at the corners of her eyes but not falling. "I know."

Then, softly: "Did… you go to the club in DC?"

The question stunned him—not because she asked, but because she asked it gently, without accusation.

He inhaled. "Yes."

Gena didn't flinch. "Did you…?"

"No," he said immediately. "Not like before."

She nodded, still not looking at him. "I don't know how to compete with the version of me that existed before… all this."

Bud stepped closer. "Gena—"

She cut him off with a soft shake of her head. No anger. Just tired truth.

"I'm not asking for details," she whispered. "I'm just… asking if you still see me in here somewhere. Under everything."

He felt something twist painfully inside him.

He placed a careful hand on her cheek. "You're still you. I promise."

She closed her eyes, leaning into the touch for a fraction of a second—an echo of the woman she used to be—then stepped back.

"We'll be okay," she said quietly. "Eventually."

Bud nodded once, though he wasn't sure if either of them believed it fully.

She returned inside, leaving Bud alone on the porch with the cold and the darkness and the quiet hum of danger.

* * *

Later that night, after everyone was asleep, Bud sat at the kitchen table reviewing his field notes. He circled discrepancies, cross-checked numbers, drew lines between farms that should've had nothing to do with each other.

One cluster kept repeating. Four Somali-run farms in three neighboring counties. All approved on the same day. All with inflated numbers. All with funding tripled. All tied to "external advisement."

He scribbled in the margin: Pattern. Not coincidence.

His phone buzzed once.

A text.

Unknown number.

Stop digging. We all have families.

Bud stared at the message until the screen dimmed.

He didn't answer. Didn't delete it. Didn't breathe for several seconds.

A long-dormant part of him—something sharp, something that had slept since Kosovo—stirred awake.

He locked the screen, set the phone down, and exhaled slowly.

Tomorrow, he would visit Hassan again. Tomorrow, he would talk to Susan. Tomorrow, he would start pulling threads.

Tonight, he sat in the dark kitchen feeling the quiet shift from peaceful to predatory.

Someone out there knew his name. Knew his number. Knew he was getting too close.

The map of his life had edges he hadn't noticed before.

And he was standing on one of them.

CHAPTER ELEVEN
Footprints

The message was still on his phone in the morning.

Stop digging. We all have families.

Bud stared at it while the coffee maker gurgled in the corner of the kitchen. The cabin was quiet—Gena still asleep, the boys not yet stirring, Moose snoring gently under the table like an old generator.

Part of him wanted to believe it was a prank.

The rest of him knew better.

People who joked didn't choose words like that. Didn't lean on family. That was leverage language. Pressure language. The kind of phrasing he'd heard before in places where consequences weren't measured in reprimand letters.

He set the phone down and poured coffee. Black. No sugar. No cream.

His hands were steady, but his chest felt tighter.

He picked the phone back up and did what came naturally.

He took a picture of the text. Backed it up. Saved it in a hidden folder.

Then turned off message previews on his lock screen.

Nobody threatened his family and got instant compliance.

Not anymore.

He was rinsing his mug when Gena came downstairs, wrapped in a thick robe, hair pulled into a loose knot. She looked tired but not shattered. Her eyes tracked him quietly.

"Morning," she said.

"Morning," Bud replied. "Sleep any?"

"A little." She hesitated. "You?"

"Enough."

She poured herself a cup of coffee, hands steadier than last week.

Progress, he told himself. Tiny steps.

"What's on your schedule today?" she asked.

"Field visits," he said. "Need to check on a few properties. Hassan's is on the list."

Her eyes flickered. "Good people."

"Yeah," Bud said softly. "Good people in a bad pattern."

She studied him a moment. "You look… keyed up."

He forced a half smile. "DC has that effect."

She didn't press. That was one of the things he loved about her when the anxiety wasn't driving everything—she knew when not to pry.

"Be careful," she said.

Always, he thought. But instead he said, "I know."

* * *

By late morning, he was back on the road leading out to the Hassan farm. The sky hung low and heavy, clouds flattening the horizon line. Snowmelt had turned the edges of the road to mud, and his truck tires chewed through with a wet growl.

As he approached the Hassan driveway, he slowed.

Something felt off.

Not a sound. Not a smell. Just a sense—the way the air changed in places where things had shifted since you'd last been there.

He pulled in and killed the engine.

No children on the porch. No chickens scratching by the coop. No smoke from the chimney.

The place looked… paused.

Bud stepped out, senses sharpening. The mud sucked at his boots as he walked toward the house. The wind was still enough that he could hear his own breath.

Halfway up the driveway, he saw them.

Tracks. Fresh ones.

Not the usual boot prints he'd expect from Hassan and his boys, who wore work boots year-round. These were harder to place—narrower, with deep, crisp edges. Two sets. Maybe three. Some lighter, some heavier. More than one vehicle had come through recently, too; he could see the tire ruts overlaying the old ones.

He crouched, fingertips brushing the impression.

Not locals. Or if they were, they weren't farmers.

Bud straightened and walked up the porch steps.

He knocked once. Waited. Knocked again, louder.

No answer.

He tried the handle.

Unlocked.

His body moved before his brain finished the argument. He stepped inside, calling out, "Hassan? It's Bud Day. Anyone home?"

Silence answered.

The kitchen smelled faintly of spices and woodsmoke, but there was an underlying scent too—cold air, like a window had been left open too long. A jacket hung on the back of a chair. A child's scarf lay crumpled on the floor.

Bud's gaze swept the room, cataloguing details without conscious effort. Two mugs in the sink. Plates on the counter. A pot on the stove, empty but not yet washed. Nothing looked overturned. No signs of struggle. Just… absence.

"Hassan?" he called again, moving down the hallway.

Bedrooms empty. Beds unmade, as if left in a hurry. The back door was bolted from the inside. No sign of the family. No note.

He stepped back out onto the porch and scanned the yard.

Then he saw it near the edge of the field—a section of fencing disturbed, the wire slightly warped. Nothing dramatic, but enough to suggest someone had leaned against it or pushed through recently.

He walked toward it, boots sucking in the mud. Beyond the fence, the ground sloped down toward a line of pines.

More tracks here.

He squatted again, tracing the impressions—men's boots, heavy tread, not the rounded, worn pattern of farm boots. He followed the trail a few yards before it disappeared into the harder, drier patch of ground beneath the trees.

He stood still. Listening.

The forest answered with the usual sounds—wind, a distant crow, branches settling.

No immediate threat.

But threat wasn't always immediate.

He pulled his phone from his pocket and took photos—of the tracks, of the disturbed fence, of the empty house. Then he dialed Hassan's number.

Straight to voicemail.

He hung up and tried again.

Nothing.

Bud's heartbeat slowed, but not in a calming way. It slowed in that deliberate, pre-incident way it always had when things started to tilt. The world narrowed—first to the farm, then to the program, then to the text on his phone.

We all have families.

"This isn't a coincidence," he murmured.

He walked back to the house and knocked on the neighbor's door—a quarter mile down the road, another small farm, older couple who'd lived there long before the state decided to get creative with grants.

The neighbor, Marlene, answered with a wary squint that softened when she recognized him.

"Oh. Mr. Day. Everything all right?"

"You seen the Hassans today?" Bud asked.

She wiped her hands on a towel. "Not since yesterday evening. Truck left early this morning. Thought they were headed to town."

"What time?"

"Sun wasn't full up yet," she said. "Maybe six? Seven?"

"Anyone else been up that way?"

She hesitated. "There was a black SUV on the road earlier. Government-looking thing. Out-of-state plates. Didn't recognize it."

Bud felt that cold line trace his spine again.

"You see who they talked to?" he asked.

"No." She shook her head. "Just saw it turning in. I mind my own business mostly."

"Have you ever seen them visit before?"

"No," she said quietly. "And I've seen a lot of government cars, Mr. Day. That one felt… different."

Bud nodded. "If you see them again, will you give me a call?"

"Is something wrong?" Marlene asked, worry creeping in.

"Just checking on things," he said. "Probably nothing."

He hated how easily the lie came out.

* * *

On the drive back toward town, he dialed Susan's number at the office.

She picked up on the second ring. "Talbot."

"It's Bud," he said. "You got a minute?"

"For you? Always."

He summarized what he'd seen—the empty house, the tracks, the neighbor's black SUV. He kept it factual, stripped of speculation.

Susan was quiet on the other end for a long moment.

"Did you call the sheriff?" she asked finally.

"Not yet," Bud said. "Not sure it's a law enforcement issue. Might be… something else."

"That 'something else' worries me more," she said.

"Me too."

"I'll check what's been logged on their file since you were in DC," she said. "See if anything moved without your signature."

"They're our farmers," Bud said. "They're under our watch."

"I know," she said. "Which is why this bothers me."

He let out a slow breath. "You think DC's moving them?"

"Relocation?" she asked. "That'd go through official channels. There'd be paperwork. You and I both know that."

"So if it's not official…"

"Then it's unofficial," she finished grimly. "And that's worse."

He could picture her in her office, pinching the bridge of her nose, eyes narrowed in that way she had when something didn't fit the patterns she'd learned to live with.

"Bud," she said quietly, "whatever you do—don't go after this alone. Not this one."

He didn't make promises for things he couldn't control. So he didn't answer that directly.

Instead he said, "Let me know what you find."

"I will. And Bud?"

"Yeah?"

"If anyone calls you about this from DC, take notes."

He almost smiled. "Always do."

When he got home, the boys were out in the yard, building what appeared to be a heavily armed snow fort. Moose supervised, occasionally stealing sticks that were meant to be flagpoles.

Gena watched from the porch; a blanket wrapped around her shoulders. She looked better in the daylight—less haunted, more anchored. When Bud pulled in, she lifted a hand.

"How'd it go?" she asked as he walked up.

"Strange," he said.

She frowned. "Strange how?"

"Hassan family wasn't home," he said. "No sign of them. Neighbor saw a black SUV with out-of-state plates this morning."

Gena's brows knitted. "That sounds… not good."

"It's probably nothing," Bud lied again, more gently this time. "But I've got calls out."

She studied his face. "You have that look."

"What look?"

"The one you had when you came back from deployments," she said softly. "Like you're mapping out exits in your head."

He exhaled a humorless breath. "Maybe."

She stepped closer, resting a hand lightly on his arm. "Just… promise me you won't chase this so hard you forget you're chasing it."

He tilted his head. "Explain."

"You get locked in," she said. "On problems. On missions. On people. You fixate until you burn yourself out."

"And you don't?" he asked gently.

She gave a small smile. "We're a matched set that way."

He covered her hand with his. "I'll be careful."

"Liar," she murmured, but there was no heat in it.

The boys shouted from the yard.

“Dad! We need artillery support!” Arnie yelled, pointing at him with a broom-turned-lance.

“Incoming,” Sly added dryly, tossing a snowball that exploded near Bud’s boots.

Somewhere between the threat on his phone, the missing Hassan family, and the black SUV tracks in the mud, Bud found himself laughing.

Gena watched him with a softness he hadn’t seen in months.

For a moment, the world narrowed to this—snow, kids, dog, wife, fatigue, warmth. And then, like always, it widened again to include danger.

* * *

That night, after the boys went to bed and Gena fell into a shallow sleep, Bud sat alone in the living room with the lights off. The clock ticked on the wall, steady and unsympathetic.

He pulled out his phone.

Scrolled past the threat text. Found Layla’s number—the one she’d quietly typed into his phone with a brief, firm instruction:

For work only. Unless it isn’t.

He hovered over it for a moment.

Then he typed:

Hassan family gone. House empty. Neighbor saw black SUV with out-of-state plates. Message last night told me to stop digging “for my family.” This smell familiar to you?

He hit send before he could talk himself out of it.

The reply came faster than he expected.

Yes. Do not go back there alone after dark. Forward me the text you received.

He sent a screenshot.

Another reply followed.

This isn't just funding fraud anymore. It's leverage. I'll start pulling what I can from my side. You keep acting normal.

He almost snorted.

Normal.

Another message popped up.

And Bud? If anyone from DC suddenly wants to "partner" on your field visits, tell me first.

His fingers moved almost of their own accord.

You always this reassuring?

A pause.

Then:

Only with people who don't know when to be scared.

He stared at the screen a long moment.

Then:

I know when. I just don't like it.

Her last message:

Good. Fear without panic is useful. Sleep if you can.

Tomorrow's going to move something.

He set the phone down on the table, her words vibrating in his mind.

Tomorrow.

Something would move.

He didn't know if that meant a piece on the board or the ground under his feet.

He only knew that the quiet in the cabin no longer felt like protection. It felt like the pause between the first warning shot and whatever came next.

CHAPTER TWELVE
The Missing

The next morning brought brittle cold and a sky the color of raw steel. Bud scraped frost off the truck windshield while his breath hung in the air like smoke. Moose watched from the porch, paws tapping anxiously at the cold wood.

Inside, Gena moved quietly through the kitchen. The boys argued softly upstairs, the way brothers do when trying not to get yelled at for waking the house too early. Everything looked normal.

Normal had never felt so fragile.

Bud drove into the Augusta office with a thermos of coffee and a knot in his stomach. He rehearsed the conversation with Susan on the way in, reminding himself to stay calm, factual, professional. The threat text still burned in the back of his mind, but he wasn't sharing that yet—not until he had a better read on who could actually be trusted inside the system.

When he walked into the building, Rick was waiting at his desk, unusually serious.

"You see the file updates?" Rick asked.

"No," Bud said. "I just got in."

Rick handed him a stack of printed forms.

Bud scanned the first page.

Hassan Grant Renewal: Status – CLOSED Reason – Beneficiary

Relocation / Program Withdrawal Official Documentation: Pending

Bud's jaw tightened.

"Relocation?" he muttered. "To where?"

"Doesn't say," Rick said. "The system updated overnight. No notification. No request. Just… closed."

Bud flipped to the next page.

Visits: No further site inspections required. Auditor Notes: None.

Reviewer: N/A. Approval Authority: Washington, DC — CODE 47B

Bud stared at that last line.

"What the hell is Code 47B?" Rick asked.

"That's not a USDA designation," Bud said. "Not one I've ever seen."

"Exactly," Rick said. "Which means someone outside our chain pushed this through."

Bud set the papers down slowly. Controlled. Deliberate. He could feel old instincts sliding into place—the way they had in Mogadishu when things didn't line up, when the map said one thing and the street said something else entirely.

He took a breath. "Anyone else's files change?"

Rick nodded. "Three. All micro-farms. All Somali-run. Same code. Same overnight closure."

Bud stood so abruptly his chair rolled back.

Rick frowned. "Bud. Don't do something stupid."

"I'm not," Bud said, though he knew that was debatable.

He walked straight to Susan's office and knocked.

"Come in," she said.

He entered. Closed the door. Sat across from her.

She took one look at him and said, "What happened?"

He slid the papers across her desk. "These updates hit overnight."

She skimmed them quickly, frown deepening with every line.

"No documentation?" she asked.

"No relocation request," Bud added. "No family contact. No field notes. And I was there yesterday. They didn't tell me a thing."

"And Code 47B?"

"Exactly."

Susan leaned back. "This isn't sloppiness. This is deliberate."

Bud nodded. "And whoever's doing it is reaching into our region without our authorization."

"And without leaving fingerprints," she added.

He hesitated. "There's more."

Susan's eyes sharpened. "What kind of more?"

"I found tracks at the Hassan property. Multiple men. Not locals. Black SUV. Neighbor confirmed."

Susan's mouth tightened. "Jesus."

"And," Bud said quietly, "I got a text last night telling me to stop digging. Mentioned family."

She froze. "Bud—why the hell didn't you lead with that?"

"Because I didn't know who to trust."

She studied him for a long, still moment. "Do you trust me?"

Bud nodded without hesitation. "Yes."

She exhaled. "Good. Because this isn't just a grant discrepancy anymore. This is bigger."

"You think I should contact law enforcement?"

Susan shook her head. "Not yet. Local law enforcement doesn't have the tools or authority for this. And if federal law enforcement is involved—either legitimately or not—we could make things worse."

Bud rubbed the back of his neck. "So what do we do?"

"For now? We gather everything. Document carefully. And tell no one who doesn't already know."

"That's you, me, Rick," Bud said.

"And?" she asked.

Bud hesitated. "And someone in DC. Someone who's been helping me see the patterns."

"I assume this is your 'contact'," she said carefully.

He nodded. "One I trust."

She didn't ask who. Smart woman.

"Alright," Susan said. "Keep them looped in. Quietly."

Bud pocketed the papers again.

"Be careful," Susan said as he stood. "There's more to lose here than a job."

* * *

He left the office at noon with a list of families to visit and a stomach full of unease. Snow had started again—flurries that danced in the wind without landing. The roads looked blurred at the edges, as if reality had started to smear.

He headed toward the next farm on his list—the Osman property. Smaller than Hassan's, tucked deeper into the woods. The drive took twenty minutes along winding roads bordered by thick pine.

Halfway there, he noticed it.

A vehicle behind him.

Black SUV. Two car lengths back. No headlights despite the gray weather. Perfectly matching his speed.

He tested it—slowed slightly.

The SUV slowed.

He accelerated around a bend.

So did they.

Bud rolled his tongue in his cheek. Not panic. Assessment.

He took a sharp right turn onto a narrow side road—one usually used by logging trucks. Hard-packed dirt. Isolated. The kind of road no GPS recommended.

SUV followed.

He breathed once. Slow. Calm.

Ahead, the road widened briefly where two old pull-offs formed a rough clearing. He signaled as if turning, slowed, and pulled into the right-hand clearing.

The SUV pulled past him, drove twenty more yards—

Then stopped.

Not long. Just enough.

Enough to mark him. Enough to let him know they saw him see them.

Then the SUV rolled forward and disappeared around the curve.

Bud sat still in the truck, fingers resting lightly on the steering wheel.

In Somalia, that move meant: We know where you are. In Kosovo, that move meant: We know who you are. In Maine, that move meant something else entirely: We can reach you anywhere.

After a moment, he exhaled slowly, backed onto the road, and continued toward the Osman property.

* * *

When he arrived, the Osman house was alive with sound—children running in and out of the doorway, chickens squawking, a goat bleating angrily at something. A stark contrast to the silence at Hassan's.

Mrs. Osman greeted him warmly. "Mr. Day! You bring the cold with you."

Bud smiled faintly. "It follows me. I try to outrun it."

She ushered him inside, offering tea, bread, warmth. Normalcy.

Her husband joined them from outside, wiping boots on the mat. "You here for the renewal paperwork?"

"In part," Bud said. "But I wanted to check on something else too."

Their eyes flickered with quiet concern but no fear.

"Have you had any visitors recently?" Bud asked.

"Only the inspector two weeks ago," Mr. Osman said.

"What inspector?"

"Man from Washington," he said. "Said he was with USDA oversight."

Bud's stomach tightened. "Name?"

"He gave one," Mr. Osman said, brow wrinkling. "But his badge didn't match the photo. I noticed it, but I did not know who to tell."

Bud breathed slowly. "What did he want?"

"To help us fill out expansion paperwork," Mrs. Osman said. "He said we qualified for more funding. But we didn't ask. And we didn't sign."

Bud felt something cold and metallic settle in his spine.

"What did he look like?" Bud asked.

"Tall," Mr. Osman said. "Bald. Scar near his eyebrow. Spoke calmly."

Bud stiffened.

Calm. Tall. Scar near the brow.

He didn't know the face yet. But he knew the type.

And he knew—without question—this was connected to Hassan's disappearance.

"Did he threaten you?" Bud asked.

They exchanged a look.

"No," Mrs. Osman said. "But he smiled too much."

Bud understood exactly what that meant.

* * *

He stayed another twenty minutes, reviewing their actual paperwork—clean, simple, honest. Nothing inflated. No suspicious signatures.

When he stepped back outside, he took a long look at the woods behind their property. Dark. Dense. A perfect place to disappear. A perfect place to… He didn't finish the thought.

As he walked back to his truck, Mrs. Osman called after him.

"Mr. Day?"

He turned.

"Is something wrong with the program?" she asked softly.

He swallowed.

Everything in him wanted to give comfort. Everything in him knew comfort was a lie.

So he said the only honest thing he could.

"I'm working on it."

She nodded slowly. "Then we will trust you."

Those words sat heavy on his chest.

Trust was weight. Weight he wasn't sure he could carry much longer.

* * *

On the drive home, he texted Layla:

SUV followed me. Hassan file closed. Osman visited by fake inspector. Need ID on Code 47B.

A few minutes later, her reply came through:

Code 47B = Internal Flag Holder Used by two agencies. Neither of them are USDA.

Bud read that twice.

Which agencies? he typed.

Layla replied:

Homeland Security. And another one I can't name over text.

He felt his pulse slow—not panic, but preparation.

Then another message:

If the SUV shows up again, do not engage. Just mark details. I'm pulling threads from this end. You pull from yours. But Bud— don't get predictable.

He stared at the phone.

Predictable. Hassan had been predictable. His drive routes were predictable. Bud's were too.

He turned onto a different road than usual. A longer way home.

Unfamiliar.

The sky had darkened now, clouds gathering into a single heavy sheet.

Snow drifted again, this time sharper, angled. The wind picked up.

As Bud rounded the last bend before the cabin, he slowed.

Tire tracks in the snow across his driveway.

Not his. Not Gena's. Not Moose's.

Fresh.

Deep.

Heading straight toward the tree line.

Bud eased off the gas.

He didn't breathe.

Didn't blink.

Didn't move for a full three seconds.

Then, quietly—out loud, but only for himself—he said:

"…something just shifted."

CHAPTER THIRTEEN
Encroachment

For a long moment, Bud just sat there at the mouth of the driveway, truck idling, eyes fixed on the tire tracks cutting across the fresh snow like a wound.

Not his. Not Gena's. Not Moose's.

The world narrowed to the geometry of intrusion: twin compressed lines entering, turning, disappearing toward the tree line along the side of the property.

He put the truck in park. Turned the engine off. Listened.

The silence was thick. Not peaceful. Not empty. Just… heavy.

Moose barked once from somewhere near the house—a short, uncertain sound, as if he wasn't sure whether to be brave or sensible.

Bud stepped out of the truck, the cold hitting him hard enough to sting.

He walked along the edge of the ruts, careful not to disturb them more than necessary.

The tracks came in from the road—same width, same spacing, same tread pattern he'd seen earlier behind him on the way to Osman's. Black SUV.

Or its twin. The tires had dug deep into the soft, half-frozen ground under the snow.

He followed the trail with his eyes.

The vehicle hadn't come straight to the cabin. It had turned off before that, cutting toward the line of pines to the right of the house—where the land dipped and the ground stayed hidden from the road.

He inhaled slowly, every sense sharpening.

This wasn't a random visitor. Delivery trucks didn't hide behind tree lines. Friends and neighbors didn't turn off before reaching the front door.

He walked closer, boots crunching softly. The air felt different near the trees—colder somehow, the way hollows always held on to winter longer than open fields.

At the edge of the pines, the SUV tracks stopped in a churn of mud and slush. The vehicle had turned around here, back and forth, enough times to blur the tread details in the middle, but the approach and exit were clear.

Footprints broke off from the muddle—two sets, maybe three, one heavier, one lighter. They curved toward the back of the property, the direction of the small trail Bud used to get to his hunting land.

He crouched, studying the impressions.

Heavy boots. Deep heel. Wide stance. The kind of walk that didn't belong to someone who spent their days behind a desk.

He felt that slow, measured calm slide into place—the one that always came just before things went sideways. The one he hadn't needed in this country in a very long time.

He stood and followed the footprints along the edge of the trees, staying to the side where the snow was less disturbed.

The tracks led toward the small rise where his truck normally sat during hunting weekends. The makeshift clearing he used as a base camp. From here, you could see a long stretch of the back pasture. From here, you could see the house.

He reached the crest of the rise and stopped.

Someone had been standing there.

The snow was stamped down in an oval, like a man had stood in one place for a long time. Boot marks layered over each other, toes pointing toward the cabin.

Watching.

Bud scanned the ground more closely.

A cigarette butt half-buried in the snow. Not a brand he recognized. Imported, maybe. The filter had a thin gold ring. Someone who cared about appearances enough to spend extra on small details. Or someone who'd spent a lot of time overseas.

He picked it up with two fingers and dropped it into his pocket.

No shells. No broken branches. No obvious markers.

They'd stood. Watched. Left.

This was a message. A calling card without the courtesy of a name.

Bud exhaled, breath fogging in front of him.

"Okay," he murmured, more to the trees than to himself. "I see you."

He followed the tracks back toward the driveway, tracing their path mentally, committing it to memory. SUV enters. Parks behind the tree line. Team dismounts. One or two walk out to his spot. Stand, observe, maybe take pictures. Then everyone leaves.

No attempt to approach the house. No attempt to contact him.

Just confirmation.

We were here. We know where you live. We know where you stand.

He walked back toward the cabin, his heartbeat steady but lower now, the way it always dipped when his mind was fully engaged.

This was familiar ground. Not Maine. Not the snow. The feeling.

The feeling of being marked.

* * *

Moose met him at the back steps, whining, tail wagging uncertainly.

"Yeah, I smell it too," Bud murmured, rubbing the dog's ears.

Inside, the cabin was warm with the smell of stew and woodsmoke. Gena was at the kitchen table, flipping through a recipe book she'd had for years, even if she rarely used it now. The boys were upstairs—he could hear them faintly, controller clicks and muffled arguing over some game.

Gena looked up as soon as he walked in.

"You're late," she said, but there was no accusation in it. Just awareness.

"Roads were slick," he said automatically.

Her eyes held his for a second too long. She'd been married to him long enough to hear the missing piece in his voice.

"Something happen?" she asked quietly.

He hesitated.

He could tell her everything—the SUV, the tracks, the fake inspector at Osman's, the missing Hassan family—but the words stacked up into a wall he wasn't ready to push onto her.

"Someone drove up earlier," she said before he could answer.

The world tightened.

"When?" he asked.

"About an hour ago," she said. "I saw the vehicle from the kitchen window. Black SUV. Tinted windows. I thought it was maybe someone lost—GPS thinks we're a through-road half the time."

"Did they come to the door?" His voice was softer now. Controlled.

"No," she said. "They pulled in, paused by the trees, then left."

"You see how many people?" he asked.

"No. I stayed inside." She paused. "I… I locked the door. Twice."

He nodded once. "Good."

"Bud," she said, voice low, "who were they?"

He weighed the options. Lying wasn't going to work—not with her. She'd spot it and spiral. Truth was heavy, but uncertainty was worse.

"I don't know yet," he said. "But they're probably connected to the Hassan program."

"Probably?" she echoed.

"Almost certainly," he admitted.

Anxiety flickered across her face, but she wrestled it down. "Are we in danger?"

He thought of the text. The SUV. The tracks.

"I don't think they'll do anything stupid while things are subtle," he said. "Right now, this is pressure. They want me nervous. Quiet."

"And are you nervous?" she asked.

"Yes," he said. "But I'm not quiet."

A tiny ghost of a smile tugged at her mouth. "That sounds like you."

He stepped closer, resting a hand on the back of her chair. "Listen. If that SUV—or any unfamiliar vehicle—comes back, you stay inside. Don't open the door. Call me, then call Susan if you can't reach me. Okay?"

She nodded. "Okay."

"And if something feels off—even if you can't say why—you take the boys to your sister's."

"That's two hours away," she said.

"That's the point," he replied.

She studied him. "It's really that serious."

"Not yet," he said. "But it's trending."

She laughed once, a dry sound. "Only you would describe danger like a weather report."

"Old habits," he said.

He moved to the window and looked out toward the trees. Nothing moved. The tracks were already starting to blur with fresh snow.

"You're going hunting this weekend?" she asked from behind him.

"That was the plan," he said.

"And now?"

He watched the tree line for another second before answering.

"And now… I'm thinking I might go a little sooner."

"To clear your head?" she asked.

"To see if they left anything else out there," he said quietly.

* * *

He waited until after dinner, after the boys had finished homework and crashed in front of a movie, after Gena had retreated upstairs with Moose to try for an early night. He waited until the house had settled into that familiar nighttime rhythm—the creaks, the low hum of the heater, the occasional muffled laugh from the boys' room.

Only then did he pull on his heavier coat and head out to the shed.

The M14 sat on its rack, oiled and ready, wood stock worn smooth by years of use. Beside it, the suppressed full auto Colt 653 Carbine and SIG 226 hung like a ghosts of another life. He took the M14 down carefully, feeling the weight settle into his hands like a handshake from an old friend.

This wasn't paranoia. This was preparation.

He slung the rifle over his shoulder, grabbed a small pack—flashlight, binoculars, extra mags, a thermos of coffee—and headed toward the back trail, boots whispering against the lightly crusted snow.

The woods swallowed him in a familiar way. Trees rose around him, tall and dark. The faint light from the cabin faded with each step until it was just him, the cold, and the rhythmic sound of his breath.

He followed the tracks again, not the SUV this time, but the human footprints. They were less distinct now, softened by fresh snowfall. But they were still there, heading toward his hunting ridge.

He moved like he had in other places, other nights—quiet, deliberate, scanning. He checked trunks for fresh scuffs, branches for broken ends, the snow for any sign of someone doubling back.

At the ridge, he crouched behind the same old stump he used as a rest when lining up long shots. From here, he could see the house—lights glowing soft in the windows, smoke rising from the chimney, everything looking impossibly ordinary.

He pulled out the binoculars.

From this vantage point, it was clear: the spot he'd seen earlier had the best line of sight on the cabin. Whoever stood here had been watching long enough to know where to stand.

He swept the binoculars slowly across the tree line.

Nothing.

Then, as he panned back toward the clearing, something small caught his eye near the base of a pine. A glint. Metal.

He moved closer, rifle slung low but not raised, every instinct humming.

Near the tree, half-buried in snow, lay a small black rectangle. The kind of thing you wouldn't notice if you weren't looking for anything at all.

He knelt and brushed away the snow.

Trail camera.

Not his.

Smaller than the ones he used. Newer. The front was scuffed, but the lens was intact. A strap had been looped around the tree trunk.

He exhaled through his teeth, equal parts impressed and furious.

They'd set up a camera. On his land. Watching his house.

He turned it over, looking for a brand. The logo was scratched off. Deliberately.

He popped the back hatch.

The SD card was still inside.

Either they hadn't had time to retrieve it yet, or they wanted him to find it empty. A little game.

He slid the card out, slipped it into an inner pocket, then closed the hatch and left the camera body where it was.

No need to let them know what he knew. Not yet.

On the way back to the house, the weight of the M14 against his shoulder felt different. Not nostalgic. Not recreational. Functional. Purposeful.

He stepped onto the porch, brushed the snow off his boots, and paused with his hand on the doorknob.

There were lines in every life—the ones you knew you'd crossed the moment your hand moved.

Tonight felt like one of those.

He went inside.

The house was warm, quiet, familiar. Boys asleep. Gena's bedroom door half-open, soft light bleeding into the hallway. Moose snoring near her feet.

Bud set the M14 in its usual place in the closet, but his mind was already somewhere else—in front of his laptop, SD card waiting.

Fifteen minutes later, he sat at the kitchen table, laptop open, card reader plugged in. The only light came from the screen, painting his face in pale blue.

He slid the card in.

Folder opened. Timestamped files.

Dozens of them.

He clicked the first one.

An image popped up—grainy, black-and-white, time-stamped two nights ago. The cabin in the distance. A faint silhouette near the porch—Gena, letting Moose out before bed.

He clicked the next.

Arnie and Sly in the yard, throwing snowballs. Moose chasing them. Bud himself crossing the frame, carrying firewood.

Another image. Another. Another.

The camera had been watching for at least forty-eight hours.

Watching all of them.

He clicked one more.

This time, the frame held something else.

In the foreground, close to the camera, a shadowed figure stood partially turned away. Tall. Broad shoulders. A glint near the right brow where the skin dipped in a familiar small crescent.

Scar.

Even in the grainy still, Bud felt his body react—a low, steady heat spreading through his chest like something old waking up.

The figure's head was turned just enough that Bud could see the hint of a profile.

Not yet a name. But a shape.

He stared at the image until the clock above the sink ticked over to midnight.

Then, very quietly, he said to the empty kitchen:

"Okay, friend. Now we're in it."

He dragged the images to a secure folder he'd set up years ago—originally for hunting footage, later repurposed for things like this. He copied them to an encrypted drive he kept hidden in a hollow behind a support beam.

He pulled out his phone.

Texted Layla.

Someone put a trail cam on my land. Watching the house. Got images. Tall male, brow scar. Black SUV matches tail from earlier. This still qualify as 'leverage' in your book?

Her reply came slower than usual.

That's escalation. Don't send the images over text. We'll find a secure way. In the meantime, assume they know your routines. Change them.

He typed:

Already started. They aren't the only ones watching now.

After a moment, her last message arrived:

Good. But remember, Bud— men like that are comfortable in the shadows. You are too. Just don't let them drag you back into a war you already survived.

He stared at her words.

Then closed the laptop, turned off the kitchen light, and stood in the dark, listening to the house breathe around him.

He'd survived two wars.

He had no idea yet what kind of war this one was going to be.

But for the first time since this started, a thin, familiar line of resolve cut through the fear.

They'd watched his family.

Now he was watching back.

And whether they knew it or not, that meant the game had changed.

CHAPTER FOURTEEN
Shadows Resolve

Bud woke before dawn, the sky still ink-dark, the house cocooned in the soft hum of sleeping bodies. He didn't need an alarm. His mind had been running long before his eyes opened.

The trail camera images sat in a folder on his encrypted drive like silent accusations.

He made coffee in the dark, not wanting to wake anyone. Moose padded in sleepily, circled once at his feet, then lay down with his head on Bud's boot as if keeping watch.

"Some help you were last night," Bud murmured.

Moose thumped his tail once in apology.

When the coffee finished brewing, Bud sat at the table again and opened the laptop. He pulled up the images—not to reexamine exposure or angle or timestamps. He'd already done all that. This time, he looked at patterns.

The scarred man had visited twice. Once around 11 p.m. Once just after 4 a.m.

Two different nights.

Two different vantage points.

Different boots. Same man.

Bud zoomed in on the fourth image. The scar ran through the right eyebrow—clean, sharp, the kind that came from glass or shrapnel. His posture was loose but deliberate, weight balanced on both feet. Comfortable in the cold. Comfortable in silence.

Professional.

Bud shifted to the timestamped metadata. Every image had the same signature embedded in the file headers.

He frowned.

Most trail cameras used generic firmware tags. These didn't.

The prefix read: LANCELOT.47B

His stomach tightened.

"Forty-seven B," he whispered.

The same override code that had closed the Hassan file.

Someone wasn't sloppy—they were arrogant.

He exhaled slowly, trying to flatten the spike of adrenaline.

He didn't know whether the message was meant to be subtle or brazen.

He only knew one thing: whoever had planted the camera believed he would find it.

And was confident enough not to care.

His phone buzzed on the table.

Layla.

Awake?

He replied: Always.

The typing bubble appeared almost immediately.

I pulled what I could on Code 47B. You're not going to like it.

He sent: Try me.

47B isn't a department. It's a classification inside one.

He waited.

Homeland Security, Counter-Fraud Division. But not the public unit. The internal one. Oversight for "sensitive partnerships."

He leaned back in his chair. "…Hell."

Her next message came quickly.

And another thing: 47B sometimes collaborates with a nameless group that handles foreign-influence investigations tied to agriculture and infrastructure. Unofficially. No public oversight. No public records. Only internal markers.

Bud typed:

That explain my scarred friend?

Yes. 47B always has field personnel. They don't wear badges. And they don't knock.

He rubbed his temple.

Why my family? Why now?

Because you saw something they didn't want seen. Because Hassan's disappearance is connected to something bigger. Because someone up the ladder thinks you're about to expose the wrong pattern.

He hesitated before typing the next question.

You're still sure this isn't just fund fraud?

A longer pause.

No. This is political cover, foreign leverage, and money— but it's also something older. Something that started years before you got assigned to Maine.

His thumb hovered over the keyboard.

How deep are you in this, Layla?

Deep enough that if I stop helping you, you're alone. Deep enough that if I help too much, I'm next. So we walk the line.

He exhaled.

Then let's walk it. What's next?

She sent three words:

Move first. Quietly.

He closed the chat window—not out of distrust, but out of focus.

This wasn't paranoia anymore. This was prep.

He pulled the SD card from the laptop, placed it in a waterproof micro-container, and hid it in the narrow space under the floorboard where he kept critical documents. The camera itself he left in the woods—unchanged, unbroken, untouched.

Let them believe he hadn't found it. Let them keep overplaying their hand.

Moose whined softly and nudged at his knee.

"Yeah," Bud murmured, "they're coming back."

And when they did, he'd be ready.

* * *

By the time the sun finally clawed its way above the pines, the cabin smelled of coffee, toast, and the kind of morning warmth that never lasted past the first crisis of the day.

Arnie ran downstairs with a hockey stick in one hand and a binder sticking halfway out of his backpack.

Sly followed slower, already irritated at the existence of morning.

Gena came down last, her robe tied too loosely, her eyes still shadowed.

She paused when she saw Bud studying the window.

"You have your thinking face on," she said.

"It's early," he replied.

"You get quieter when something's wrong," she said simply.

He almost smiled. "And you get louder."

She returned the half-smile. "Marriage is balance."

"Boys," Bud said, "finish up. I'll drive you today."

That caught Gena's attention.

"You always drive them," she said carefully, "when you need to keep an eye on something outside."

He paused.

She wasn't wrong.

"Just want to get out early," he said.

Gena stepped closer, lowering her voice. "Bud… did something happen last night? You barely slept."

He kept his gaze on the window. "Tracks in the driveway. Someone came by before I got home."

Her breath hitched. "Them?"

"Probably," he said. "But they didn't approach."

"That doesn't make it better."

"I know."

She swallowed. "Do we need to… leave? Stay somewhere else? For a few days?"

Her asking that—Gena, who clung to routine like rope—told him exactly how frightened she truly was.

"No," he said gently. "Moving makes us easier to track. Here, I know the terrain."

"And you have rifles hidden under every third floorboard," she said lightly, but her voice shook.

"Just the important ones," he corrected.

She pressed her lips together. "Please be careful."

He rested a hand on her arm. "Always."

But when he looked back at the window, he had a sudden, undeniable certainty:

They weren't watching him anymore. They were watching all of them.

* * *

The drive to the boys' school was uneventful. Too uneventful.

The same black sedan from yesterday wasn't behind him today, but a silver crossover kept a steady distance for far too many intersections.

Might be coincidence. Might be pattern. Maine didn't have heavy traffic in the morning—people tended to stick out if they stuck around.

When he turned into the school lot, the crossover continued straight.

Sly raised an eyebrow. "You're doing the mirror thing again."

"What mirror thing?" Bud asked.

"You checked every car on the drive here," Sly said flatly. "Twice. And you always do that when Mom's upset or when you're planning something you don't want to talk about."

Arnie chimed in, "Or when you're about to take the M14 out on a 'walk.'"

Bud blinked. "When did you two get that observant?"

Sly muttered, "We have eyes."

Arnie added, "And we're not dumb."

Bud gave them both a tired smile. "Well… keep those eyes open. If anything weird happens at school, you find a teacher. And call me."

"Define weird," Sly said.

"Anyone asking your last name," Bud answered.

Arnie's face paled almost imperceptibly. Sly stiffened.

"Dad…" Sly said slowly, "what's going on?"

Bud leaned back. "Nothing you need to worry about yet. But keep your head on a swivel. Both of you."

They nodded, not reassured but obedient.

When they got out and jogged toward the school entrance, Moose whined from the back seat—today he'd insisted on coming along.

Bud scratched the dog behind the ears. "You too. Keep the house safe."

Moose barked once. Determined. Small. But real.

Bud didn't feel reassured, but somehow that helped.

* * *

On the drive back, he took the long way—through back roads, then a quick cut toward the old logging route. The SUV from yesterday didn't appear, but the absence felt just as deliberate.

He parked near the trailhead he used during fall hunting season. Not to hunt. To watch.

He used the M14's scope to scan the tree line behind his property from a distance. The light wind stirred the branches, but nothing moved that shouldn't.

He checked the ridge again.

Still nothing.

But someone had been here. And someone would be back.

He should go to the sheriff. He should tell Gena everything. He should send the boys to their aunt's.

But every instinct—every downrange lesson—told him those moves made targets bigger, not smaller.

Predictable reactions. Predictable fear. Predictable patterns.

He had to break his own pattern before someone else broke his family.

He took out his phone and texted Layla:

Need secure way to send images. You have one?

Her reply:

Yes. There's a drop location. You'll go tonight. Alone.

He typed:

Instructions?

When you're ready. And Bud— they will escalate again. Be ahead of it.

He stared at the message for a long time.

Then he put the phone away and drove home.

But as he turned into the driveway, he noticed one more thing:

Fresh footprints near the porch. Not Gena's. Too large to be either boy's. And Moose's paws weren't near them.

Bud killed the engine.

Got out slowly.

Walked toward the prints.

They led to the porch.

Stopped.

Then turned around.

No knock. No message. Just silent acknowledgment:

We can get closer.

Bud closed his eyes for a second, that old weight of inevitability settling on his shoulders.

He whispered the words he rarely allowed himself to say:

"…this is gonna get bad."

And then he went inside.

CHAPTER FIFTEEN
Closer Than the Trees

By late afternoon the sky had gone that dim pewter color that meant snow was thinking about falling but hadn't committed yet. Bud stood at the edge of the porch, staring at the fresh footprints that did not belong to anyone who should have been here.

Big. Deliberate. No hesitation in the stride.

A man comfortable on unfamiliar terrain.

Bud crouched, checking spacing, depth, and direction.

Heavy boots. Same approximate weight distribution as the prints at the trail-cam site. Same length. Same tread.

Scarred Man had been close enough to touch the cabin door.

No knock. No noise. No message except his presence.

A reminder.

A warning.

A claim.

Bud's breath condensed in a long, slow exhale.

"Bud?" Gena's voice trembled behind him. "What happened?"

He turned. She was wrapped in a thick sweater, hands worried into the sleeves, her eyes pinned to his face as if reading a verdict.

"Someone was here," he said quietly. "Earlier. Not long before I got back."

Her breath tightened. "Someone from—your work?"

"Someone connected to it," he said. "They didn't try to get in. Just… looked."

"Looked?" she echoed. "At what?"

He scanned the porch, the windows, the darkened edge of the woods.

"At us," he said softly.

Gena swayed slightly, catching herself on the railing. "This isn't farm grants, Bud. This is—this is something else."

"I know," he said, stepping closer. "And I'm handling it."

"No," she whispered, shaking her head. "This time you're lying to me. I can hear it."

He paused.

Gena leaned her forehead into her palm. "Every time you go quiet, it means you're carrying something alone."

"Because I don't want to put weight on you," Bud said.

"Bud," she said, voice cracking, "you're not protecting me by shutting me out. You're terrifying me."

He exhaled. "I'm sorry."

Her voice softened, trembling at the edges. "Just tell me—are we in danger?"

"Yes," he said honestly. "But not helpless."

She closed her eyes, breathing through the answer.

"And the boys?" she asked.

Bud's jaw clenched. "I won't let anything touch them."

"That's not a plan," she whispered. "That's a prayer."

He had no answer for that.

Moose pressed his head against Gena's leg, sensing her spiraling. She leaned down and stroked the dog's back with shaking fingers.

Bud rested a hand on her shoulder. "I'll keep the boys close. Doors locked. Lights on. And tonight, I'm heading out for a short while."

Her head snapped up. "Out where?"

He paused. "A drop location."

Gena blinked. "Like… intelligence stuff?"

Bud hesitated. Then nodded once. "Something like that."

"And you're doing this alone?" she asked.

"Someone needs to," he said.

"No," she whispered. "Someone shouldn't."

But he stepped forward and kissed her forehead, gently. "I'll be back before midnight."

"Bud—" she reached for his arm, but he slipped out of her grip gently.

"Stay inside," he said.

And then he left, Gena watching from the doorway with fear tracing the edges of her silhouette.

* * *

He drove a long loop before heading to the actual location Layla sent—checking mirrors, watching shadows, making slow, deliberate turns to flush out any tail.

Nothing obvious.

But absence didn't always mean safety.

Layla's instructions had been precise:

Follow Route 11 past the old mill. Turn off before the bridge. There's a trailhead with a rusted plow. Park. Walk one-third mile north along the riverbank. You'll find a red mailbox nailed to a fallen birch. Place the drive inside. Leave immediately. Do not linger.

It was almost nostalgic. A dead-drop without the theatrics.

It felt familiar.

The trailhead was empty when he arrived. The rusted plow listed to one side like a dying animal, half-swallowed by weeds. Snow crunched beneath his boots as he walked the river path, following the sound of water under thin ice.

The birch lay half-fallen, stripped of bark on one side. The red mailbox was there, battered, paint peeling.

Bud flipped the lid.

Empty.

Good.

He removed the encrypted drive, placed it inside, and closed the lid quietly.

The moment he stood, he felt the shift.

Not sound. Not movement. Just a prickle at the back of his neck—the kind that came when someone else was in your perimeter.

He scanned the tree line casually, letting his eyes drift as if admiring the woods.

Nothing.

But he knew. Someone was there.

He walked back toward the truck at an unhurried pace, posture relaxed, breath steady. He didn't speed up, didn't look over his shoulder, didn't reach for a weapon.

That was how you told predators you weren't prey.

Halfway to the truck, his phone buzzed.

Layla.

Drop received. Now listen carefully. You need to go home.

Immediately. Do not take the same road back.

Bud stopped.

Typed:

Why?

A pause. Then:

Because someone else just accessed the drop zone three minutes after you did. And I don't think they were on our side.

Bud swallowed.

Typed:

Scarred man?

Yes. And he wasn't alone.

Bud's blood turned to ice.

He looked back toward the woods.

Nothing moved.

But now he knew they weren't just watching anymore.

They were stalking.

* * *

He took a different route home—back roads winding through thickets of fir and frozen bogland. He checked mirrors reflexively, but the danger wasn't behind him.

It was ahead.

When he pulled into the cabin driveway, the porch light was on. Warm. Soft. Normal.

But something was wrong.

Moose was barking. Inside the house.

Not frantic. Warning.

Bud hurried up the steps and opened the door.

Gena stood in the kitchen, white as a sheet, one hand gripping the back of a chair, the other pressed against her chest. Her breath came shallow, sharp. Her eyes were locked on the living room window.

"What happened?" Bud demanded.

Gena pointed—hand trembling—to the glass.

Bud crossed the room in two strides.

There, taped to the outside of the window with a strip of gray duct tape, was a single sheet of paper.

No words.

Just a picture.

Printed. Black-and-white.

Bud leaned closer.

His stomach dropped.

The photo was from the trail camera he'd found. But not one he had opened.

It showed Bud in the kitchen earlier that morning, coffee mug in hand, looking into the distance with a solemn, unreadable expression.

And beneath the image, someone had drawn—by hand—a small circle around his head.

Not a crosshair. Not overly theatrical.

Just a reminder:

We see you. We choose the moment. Not you.

Gena made a strangled sound behind him. "Bud… what does that mean?"

Bud didn't trust his voice.

He peeled the picture off the glass, folded it once, then again until the image was hidden. He slipped it into his jacket pocket.

"We're okay," he said quietly.

Gena looked ready to break. "We're not okay."

"I'll handle it," he said.

"No," she whispered, stepping toward him. "I'm drowning, Bud. The boys see it. You see it. And now strangers—men—are watching us in our own house. You say you'll handle it, but I don't even know what 'it' is anymore."

Bud cupped her face gently. "Gena, listen to me. You and the boys are my priority. Always."

"What about you?" she whispered. "Do you even care what happens to yourself?"

He didn't answer.

He couldn't.

Instead, he kissed her forehead—light, steady, familiar.

"I need you to take the boys to your sister's tomorrow," he said. "Just for a few days."

"And leave you here alone?" she asked, voice cracking.

"It's safer," he said.

"For us?" she asked.

"For everyone," he replied.

Her eyes filled with tears. "You can't fight ghosts, Bud."

He looked toward the tree line.

"No," he said softly. "But ghosts can bleed."

Gena flinched.

He didn't take the words back.

* * *

That night, after the house finally settled into a restless quiet, Bud sat at the table with the folded picture in front of him. He placed a small black notebook beside it—the one he hadn't opened in ten years.

His war notebook. The one he'd used for sightlines, threat patterns, extraction timing.

He flipped to a clean page.

Wrote three names:

Hassan (missing) Osman (fake inspector) 47B (override)

Then a fourth:

Scarred Man

He added a question mark beside it.

Not out of uncertainty. Out of discipline.

Only confirmed patterns went into the notebook without question marks.

He wrote another line beneath it:

They're testing boundaries. Test back.

He closed the notebook.

Pulled out his phone.

Texted Layla:

They left a photo. From the trail cam. On my window. Marked.

Layla responded almost instantly.

Bud. Listen. This is a psychological play. Escalation. But not the final move. They want you off-balance. Don't give them what they want.

He replied:

Already passed that point. Next steps?

Her response:

Tomorrow, we start pulling threads. You gather everything local. I'll handle DC. But Bud— after tonight, nothing is casual anymore.

He typed:

Was it ever?

Her last reply before he set the phone down:

Not for men who survive wars. This is just a different battlefield.

Bud looked toward the dark window, the reflection of the room faint against the black mirror of night.

Somewhere out there, Scarred Man was waiting. Watching. Choosing the moment.

Bud breathed once, steady and low.

He could feel the shift inside himself—the threshold crossed not by choice, but by necessity.

He wasn't just reacting anymore.

He was preparing.

And for the first time since this started, he didn't feel hunted.

He felt engaged.

CHAPTER SIXTEEN
Fault Lines

Bud didn't sleep. Not for a minute.

He lay in the dark beside Gena, listening to every sound the cabin made—every wooden pop as the temperature dropped, every shift of Moose at the foot of the bed, every faint rustle outside the window.

The scarred man wasn't out there. Not tonight. Bud was almost certain.

Tonight's danger wasn't external.

It was inside the house.

Beside him, Gena trembled in her sleep—small quivers, like someone caught halfway between a nightmare and a panic attack. Twice he reached to touch her shoulder, to soothe her back into deeper breathing. Twice she startled, then clung to his hand.

"Don't leave," she whispered once, not fully awake.

"I won't," he said softly.

She relaxed enough to drift again, but the tension didn't leave her body. It vibrated through her, the way electrical current hums through old wires.

Bud watched her in the faint glow from the hallway nightlight.

She was breaking. Or had already broken and was trying to hold the pieces together with sheer will.

When the first blue tint of dawn slid across the room, Bud slipped out of bed and dressed quietly. Jeans, flannel, undershirt, boots. He moved like he did in deployment tents—efficient, silent, aware.

Downstairs, he made coffee and warmed the house. The snow outside had thickened into a gray blur, muting all sound.

Gena came downstairs twenty minutes later, wearing a coat over her pajamas. Her eyes were red, hair messy, but she looked steadier than last night.

"Coffee?" Bud asked.

She shook her head. "Packed the boys' things already."

"So you're going," he said.

She nodded once. "It feels wrong to leave, but it feels worse to stay."

"Good," Bud said softly.

"Good?" she echoed.

"You're protecting them," he said. "That's what matters."

Gena bit her lip. "What about you?"

"I'll be fine."

She looked at him—really looked. "You say that the way people say 'I love you' when they've already decided to leave."

Her words hit harder than the threat text.

He crossed to her, took her hands gently. "Gena. I'm not leaving. I'm clearing the field."

"What does that even mean?" she asked.

"It means I'm not letting this come into our home again," he said.

"Again?" she repeated. "What—what exactly came into our home?"

Bud opened his mouth to answer.

He didn't get the chance.

A loud knock rattled the front door.

Gena jumped like she'd been shot.

Bud stiffened—not visibly, not dramatically, but enough that the air around him changed. His posture straightened, shoulders squared, jaw tightening. A shift only someone who'd lived with him through war and after-war would notice.

"Stay back," he murmured.

Gena grabbed the counter and held on.

Bud moved to the door. Quiet. Controlled.

He didn't open it immediately. Checked the peephole first.

A delivery driver stood on the porch, holding a sealed cardboard box and shivering in the cold.

Bud opened the door halfway. "Morning."

"Package for… Day. B. Day."

"That's me."

"Need a signature," the man said.

Bud signed. The driver handed the package over and rushed back to his truck, eager to escape the cold.

Bud closed the door, eyeing the box.

No sender listed. No branding.

He carried it to the table. Gena hovered, pale.

"Bud… don't."

"It's fine," he said.

It wasn't fine.

But the box was light. Not explosive-light—document-light.

He slit the tape with his pocketknife.

Inside was a single manila envelope.

No note.

No return address.

No fingerprints that he could see.

He slid out the contents.

Pictures.

Twenty of them.

All printed.

All from the same trail camera.

But these were different.

These weren't shots of Bud or his family.

These were shots taken facing the opposite direction—as if the camera had been rotated intentionally.

And in several frames, partially obscured by trees, a figure appeared.

Tall. Broad. Scar near the brow.

Scarred Man.

Watching Bud's ridge. Watching the path. Watching the cabin.

The angles were perfect—taken from distances that made him nearly invisible unless you knew what to look for.

And in the final photo, Scarred Man wasn't in shadow anymore.

He stood in the clearing, looking directly into the camera lens, expression calm. Not threatening. Not aggressive.

Just… present.

Bud exhaled.

Gena covered her mouth.

"What does that mean?" she whispered.

"It means he's not hiding," Bud said.

"That doesn't make me feel better," she whispered.

"It shouldn't," Bud murmured.

He gathered the photos, set them aside, and pulled out his phone.

Texted Layla:

Received package. Photos taken by the scarred man's team. Deliberate. He wants me to know he's close.

Layla replied almost instantly:

This is a "territory" message. They're telling you the land around you belongs to them now. This is escalation phase two.

Bud typed:

Phase two leads where?

A pause.

Then:

Phase three is direct confrontation. Not necessarily lethal. Just unavoidable. Be ready for it.

Bud's jaw tightened.

He looked at the cabin interior—fireplace, photos of the boys, Gena's coat still draped over her chair.

He typed:

Gena and boys leaving for sister's today.

Layla's reply came fast:

Good. Their presence ties your hands. You don't need tied hands right now.

Bud didn't disagree.

* * *

The boys thundered downstairs a few minutes later, backpacks overstuffed, Moose excitedly weaving between their legs. Arnie wore his hockey jacket. Sly carried his tablet like it was a limb.

"You guys ready to go?" Bud asked.

Arnie nodded. "Are we really staying at Aunt Maria's?"

"Yes," Gena said before Bud could answer. "Just for a few days."

"Is this about the weird SUV?" Sly asked.

Gena faltered.

Bud stepped in. "It's about giving Mom a break from all the noise here. And giving you two a change of scenery."

Sly stared at him. Arnie too.

Neither believed him, but both accepted the lie for Gena's sake.

Gena hugged the boys one at a time, harder than usual. She grabbed her overnight bag, swallowed hard, and turned to Bud.

"Please," she whispered. "Don't do anything reckless."

He kissed her—light, brief, familiar.

"Drive safe," he said.

"I will."

She hesitated at the door.

"Bud… come with us."

He shook his head. "I can't."

She didn't argue. Didn't cry. Didn't plead.

That scared him more than anything else could have.

She nodded once, quietly devastated, and led the boys outside.

Bud watched the car pull away, disappearing down the snowy road until the taillights became faint red ghosts and then nothing at all.

The house felt too big. Too empty.

Too vulnerable.

He turned back to the table. Looked at the pictures again.

Scarred Man had stood thirty yards from his ridge. Then twenty. Then ten. Then here, staring into a camera he knew Bud would find.

This wasn't surveillance.

This was rhythm. Pacing. Testing. Measuring Bud's reaction time.

Bud picked up the last photo again.

Scarred Man's eyes were unreadable. Not mocking. Not angry.

Just evaluating.

Bud whispered, "You think you know me."

He placed the photo face-down.

Then he went to the closet and pulled out the M14. Checked chamber. Checked action. Loaded a magazine. Set it by the door.

Next, he retrieved a small canvas pack from the garage—one he hadn't used in years. 4 7.62 Magazines, 6 5.56 magazines, Medical kit. Paracord. Flashlight. Multitool. Batteries. Water pouch.

He felt the old rhythm settle into his bones.

He texted Layla:

When does phase three usually happen?

Her reply came quick:

When they're certain you're alone.

He typed one more message:

Then they'll be here soon.

Layla responded:

Yes. But remember— phase three isn't the last phase. It's the invitation. You decide whether you accept it.

Bud didn't reply.

He set the phone aside.

Put on his coat.

Stepped outside.

The snow had begun falling harder now—thick flakes drifting silently through the air, settling on the porch railing, softening the world.

Across the tree line, something shifted.

Not movement. Not sound.

Just pressure.

Presence.

Bud's pulse slowed—not with fear, but with familiarity. He had lived enough years in enough hostile places to recognize when an adversary was within one hundred yards.

He raised his voice—not loud, not aggressive, but controlled.

"You've been watching," he said to the woods. "Now I'm watching back."

The snow absorbed his words, swallowing them whole.

Bud waited.

A long moment passed.

Then—so faint he wasn't sure it was real—a glimmer broke the tree line.

Metal? Glass? Binoculars?

Or eyes catching the faintest light?

Bud didn't reach for the rifle.

He didn't step forward.

He simply stood still and allowed the silence to acknowledge both of them.

A handshake neither wanted, but both understood.

Finally, the glimmer faded.

Bud let the breath leave his lungs slowly, his resolve sharpening into something cold and clean.

He texted Layla again:

He's here.

Layla replied:

Then it begins now. Your next step matters. Don't let him set the rhythm. You set it.

Bud put the phone away, the snow continuing to fall around him like the quiet before impact.

He was no longer waiting for the next move.

He was making one.

And Scarred Man, wherever he stood in the pines, seemed to sense it.

CHAPTER SEVENTEEN
The Man in the Pines

Snow muffled everything—sound, distance, reason. Thick flakes drifted sideways across the clearing as if the weather had conspired with Scarred Man to blur edges, conceal movement, and slow thought.

But Bud's thoughts weren't slow.

They were sharper than they'd been in years.

He stood at the edge of the porch, boots planted, breath steady. He could feel it—like pressure behind his sternum, like the faint electric tingle he used to get before a bad door was about to open overseas.

Someone was in the woods. Standing. Watching. Waiting for him to move.

"Alright," Bud murmured, barely audible above the wind. "Let's see who you really are."

He stepped off the porch.

Not rushing. Not creeping. Just walking—quiet, purposeful, as if the snowstorm were nothing more than a late-season inconvenience.

He moved down the driveway, stopping halfway between the cabin and the tree line. The heavy pines to his right curved inward, forming a shallow U-shaped hollow where shadows collected.

Bud scanned it with the same methodical sweep he used in Mogadishu alleyways and Kosovo forests: Left to right. Top to bottom. Slow. Consistent. Unblinking.

Nothing moved.

But something was there. His body knew it before his mind did.

"You don't need to hide," Bud said. Not loud—just projected, carried by the wind. "You already introduced yourself."

A pause. A shift of air. And then—almost impossibly quiet—the faint crunch of a boot on fresh snow.

A figure stepped out from between the pines.

Tall. Still. Deliberate.

Scar under the right brow. Paracord bracelet wrapped around a gloved wrist. Jacket the kind you wore in countries whose names didn't appear in newspapers. No visible weapon—but the absence meant nothing.

The man stopped twenty yards away, posture relaxed but not careless.

He didn't look like a thug. He didn't look like a bureaucrat.

He looked like someone who had survived long enough to be neither.

Bud didn't move. Didn't speak.

He let the silence test them both.

Finally, Scarred Man inclined his head once—almost polite.

"Mr. Day."

His voice was low, smooth, accented in a way that suggested he'd learned English from multiple instructors and continents.

Bud's jaw tightened. "You know my name."

"I know your file," the man said. "And your habits. And your record."

"That a threat?"

"Acknowledgment," Scarred Man replied. "You've earned respect."

Bud kept his stance neutral. "Then why are you stalking my land?"

A faint smile ghosted across the man's mouth. "Stalking implies hostility. I prefer the term 'assessment.'"

Bud glared. "My family isn't part of your assessment."

Scarred Man's eyes flicked toward the cabin and back. "They were never in danger."

"You and I have different definitions of danger."

The man nodded again—slight, thoughtful. Snow gathered on his shoulders as if afraid to melt.

"Perhaps," he said. "But understand this, Mr. Day. If I wanted to walk through your front door, I would have. If I wanted to harm you, I would not have delivered the camera images. I am not your enemy."

Bud barked a humorless laugh. "You show up on my land at night and drop surveillance on my window. You want to convince me you're a friend?"

"I want to convince you that we share a problem," Scarred Man said evenly.

Bud's pulse hitched—but he didn't show it.

"You took the Hassans," Bud said quietly.

The man blinked once. "No. But I know who did."

Bud felt heat rise in his chest. "Where are they?"

"Safe," Scarred Man said. "For now."

"That's not good enough."

"It is better than the alternative."

Bud stepped forward, closing the distance to fifteen yards. The man didn't flinch. Not even a muscle twitch.

"Who has them?" Bud demanded.

Scarred Man tilted his head. "You think it's political corruption. A funding scheme. Maybe foreign influence. And you're not wrong."

"But?" Bud pressed.

"But you're missing the oldest piece," the man said. "The one that started a decade before you ever touched a grant application."

Bud's heart thudded once. Hard.

The Woods around them suddenly felt too quiet.

"What piece?" Bud asked.

Scarred Man didn't answer immediately. Instead, he studied Bud as if deciding whether to hand him a weapon or a burden.

Finally: "Do you remember Mogadishu, Mr. Day?"

Every nerve in Bud's body went taut.

"You were there," Bud said, voice low, not a question.

"Not as a rebel combatant," the man said. "Not then. But I was there when certain events unfolded. Events involving men who believed they were doing the right thing for their families. Events involving a boy who watched Americans take down the men who fed him. Events that changed trajectories."

Bud's breath froze mid-exhale.

"There were hundreds of boys," he said. "Thousands."

Scarred Man nodded faintly. "Yes. But only one watched you drag three wounded Rangers behind a burning technical truck. Only one saw you leave food with a dying woman in a collapsed house. Only one remembered your face."

A silence descended—heavy, cavernous, pulling the world inward.

Bud's throat felt tight. "Tell me his name."

"You already know it," the man said.

Bud whispered: "Aden."

Scarred Man finally smiled—small, cold, almost proud.

"I told you. I am not your enemy."

Bud felt the world tilt slightly. "Then what are you?"

The man stepped forward to thirteen yards—close enough that Bud could see the jagged texture of the scar under his eyebrow.

"I am the man sent to contain the consequences," he said. "The consequences of men who made promises in Somalia and funded operations that never ended. The consequences of factions who came to America through back doors. The consequences of debt."

Bud shook his head slowly. "What does that have to do with the Hassan family? They're good people."

"Yes," Scarred Man agreed. "And Aden respects good people. That is why he moved them before the others could."

Bud's mind raced. "The others?"

Scarred Man inhaled slowly. "Mr. Day… the funding fraud is not about money. It's about placement. Control. Leverage. The farms are assets. Cover operations. This isn't new. It didn't start in Maine. It didn't start in Minnesota. It didn't even start in Africa."

"Then where?" Bud asked.

The man's eyes glinted with something like sadness.

"In the American agencies that used Somali intermediaries long after they should have severed ties."

The wind shifted. Hard. Cold. Snow gusted between them.

"Why warn me?" Bud asked.

"Because you are already in the field," Scarred Man said. "And because Aden does not want to kill you. He sees you as… unfinished business. A loose thread from a chapter he has not accepted."

Bud stared. "He's targeting my family to get to me."

"No," the man said firmly. "If he wanted them harmed, they would have been harmed. The surveillance was not from him. Aden is one of three factions now engaged."

"Three," Bud repeated. "Let me guess—the one you represent isn't the worst one."

"We don't kill families," the man said simply.

Bud didn't thank him.

The man continued, "Take your wife and sons far from here."

"They already left."

"Good," the man said. "Keep them gone."

"They'll come back," Bud said.

"You misunderstand," Scarred Man replied. "Keep them gone. Permanently. You cannot fight this and protect them."

Bud's jaw clenched. "I'm not abandoning my family."

"Then they will die," the man said with the calm of someone stating weather forecasts.

Bud felt something cold coil in his gut.

"Why me?" Bud asked. "Why here? Why now?"

The man exhaled once, slow, measured.

"Because, Mr. Day… you were the first American Aden ever respected."

Silence again.

Heavy. Old.

"Where is he?" Bud asked.

Scarred Man shook his head. "I can't tell you yet."

"Then what do you want from me?"

"For now? One thing." The man stepped back into the shadows of the pines, presence thinning. "Stop trying to solve this alone. The next wave won't be surveillance. It will be contact. Direct. Controlled. And you will fail without help."

Bud stepped forward. "You offering help?"

"I am offering a warning," the man said. "There will come a moment when you will have to choose whether to pull the trigger."

Bud's voice went low. "Why? Because he won't?"

"Because he will," the man said softly.

And then he vanished. Not abruptly. Not dramatically.

Just… absent. As if he'd never been there.

Bud stood in the falling snow, breath fogging the air, mind racing.

He turned slowly and walked back toward the cabin.

Inside, the house felt hollow without the boys. Too quiet. Too still.

He closed the door behind him, leaned against it, and let the last five minutes replay in his mind.

Aden. Alive. Involved. Targeting farms. Moving families. Running an operation through three factions. And sending his most disciplined man to warn Bud.

Bud wasn't rattled.

He was something else entirely.

Engaged.

He walked to the kitchen, grabbed his notebook, and opened it to a clean page.

He wrote:

**Aden alive. Ops in Maine tied to earlier Somalia ops. Hassan moved for protection (which means risk = high). Three factions involved:

Aden's

Scarred Man's (stability?)

Unknown (violent?)**

Then, beneath it:

Next step: Force clarity. Stop reacting. Start hunting.

He closed the notebook.

Checked the M14.

Checked the Colt Carbine.

Checked the Sig.

Checked every window.

Then he texted Layla:

Just made contact. Long story. We need to talk. Not over text. Tomorrow. Same summit location. This time parking garage level 3. No badge. No phone. Just you.

Layla replied seconds later:

Understood. Be prepared—someone else will try to make contact before then. This isn't over. This is the start.

Bud locked the door and finally let exhaustion settle through him.

Tomorrow the board would tilt again. Tomorrow lines would be drawn.

Tomorrow names would be spoken out loud.

But tonight, he whispered the last words Scarred Man said, letting them burn into him:

There will come a moment when you will have to choose whether to pull the trigger.

Bud set the rifle beside the bed and whispered back:

"…I've already chosen."

CHAPTER EIGHTEEN
Level Three

The parking garage beneath the hotel smelled like wet concrete, old oil, and bad coffee. Fluorescent lights hummed overhead, flickering just enough to make the shadows feel alive.

Bud turned the wheel and descended to Level Three.

He'd parked in this garage a dozen times for conferences, briefings, and oversight summits. It had never felt this quiet.

He backed into a spot near a concrete pillar. Not against a wall—that was a trap if someone boxed you in. Not dead center—that made you a beacon. Somewhere in between. Options.

He cut the engine and sat for a moment, watching the rearview mirror. No vehicles followed him in. No delayed entries. No doors slamming in the distance.

Just the slow drip of water from a pipe and the thump of his own heartbeat.

His phone was off, battery removed, SIM card in a faraday sleeve under the seat. The only electronics on him were a cheap analog watch and a key fob. No M14 today. No Sig. He was in DC. Different rules.

Different battlefield.

He stepped out of the rental car, closed the door quietly, and slipped the key into his coat pocket. His footsteps echoed softly as he moved toward the central aisle, eyes flicking over every parked car, every blind corner.

A black sedan sat near the ramp, dustier than the rest. Haven't moved in days.

A grey SUV with government plates. Might be someone's real ride. Might be something else.

He catalogued it all without thinking.

Then he saw her.

Layla stood near a support column halfway down the lane, hands in her coat pockets, hair pulled back into a loose knot. She wasn't looking at him at first—she was watching the ramp, the way people came and went. Checking lines of sight. Seating herself in the geometry of risk.

Not a civilian.

Not really.

Bud walked toward her, pace steady, shoulders loose. When he drew close enough, she finally turned.

"Ben," she said quietly.

"Layla."

No automatic smiles. No pleasantries. Just names. Acknowledgment.

"You walked," he observed.

"I parked a block away and came in through the pedestrian entrance," she said. "Less traceable."

"Anyone behind you?"

"If there was," she replied, "they didn't want me to know it."

He nodded.

"Show me," she said.

He didn't ask what. She knew why they were here.

He pulled a small, flat flash drive from his inside coat pocket—the duplicate of the one he'd left in the red mailbox. The one with the trail-cam footage and Scarred Man's face.

He handed it over.

Layla took it with a care that bordered on reverence. Not for the object—for what it represented.

She slipped it into a narrow, shielded sleeve in her bag. "I'll get this into a clean system. No agency network. I have access to a secure node that won't flag traffic unless we make noise."

"Isn't that," Bud said drily, "exactly what we're doing?"

"Not yet," she replied. "Right now, we're just… listening."

Bud exhaled through his nose. "You said 47B works with a 'nameless group' on foreign influence. How nameless are we talking?"

"The kind that doesn't have a website," Layla said. "No FOIA footprint. No public budget line. When they travel, they use other agencies' cover."

"Scarred Man?" Bud asked.

She nodded. "Almost certainly."

"He says he's not my enemy. Says Aden moved the Hassan family to keep them safe from 'the others.'"

Layla's eyes sharpened. "He told you Aden's name?"

"He didn't have to," Bud said quietly. "I knew it."

Layla watched him for a beat. "You want to tell me how?"

"No," Bud said. "But I will. Eventually."

She accepted that.

"But if Aden is moving families like chess pieces," Layla said, "then our little funding irregularities are part of a much bigger board."

"Bigger how?"

Layla leaned one shoulder against the pillar, keeping half her body angled outward so she could see both the ramp and Bud. "We've seen something like this pattern before. Ten, fifteen years ago. Different region. Different diaspora. Same structure."

"Let me guess," Bud said. "Money through charities. Grants as cover. Small businesses as shells."

"Yes," she said. "With one twist. The real power wasn't in the money. It was in the data."

Bud frowned. "What data?"

"Land records. Ownership data. Proximity to critical infrastructure. Transportation routes. Food distribution channels. You know how we talk about 'food deserts' in urban planning? Now imagine someone mapping strategic food choke points."

Bud felt that cold coil twist in his gut. "Weaponizing the food chain."

"Or just holding it," Layla said. "Waiting. Building leverage for a moment when starving the right place at the right time could break a district, a state… a response posture."

"Who would try that?"

"Anyone patient enough to play on a fifteen-year clock," she said.

He thought of Mogadishu. Held the image in his mind—the boy in the alley. The eyes that watched everything.

"Aden is patient," Bud said.

Layla didn't ask how he knew.

"And the scarred one?" she asked. "Did he say who he answers to?"

"No," Bud said. "He wants to 'contain consequences.' That's what he called it. He told me I can't fight this and protect my family at the same time."

"He's not wrong," Layla said softly.

Bud winced.

She didn't apologize.

"I sent Gena and the boys to her sister's," he said. "For now."

"For now is not a plan," Layla said.

She said it gently, but it still landed like a strike.

He nodded once. "Scarred Man said there are three factions. His. Aden's. And a third he wouldn't name. My guess? The third is the one who wrote that text about 'we all have families.'"

Layla's eyes darkened. "That tracks."

"You know who they are," Bud said.

"I know who they might be," she corrected. "There's a cluster in the data that smells like a certain… overfunded, under-supervised domestic unit."

"Agency?" Bud asked.

She shook her head. "Not exactly. Think of them as subcontractors who got too cozy with their patrons. The kind of people you send when you want pressure without paperwork."

"Mercs?" Bud said.

"More like deniable enforcement," she said. "They wear badges when it's convenient. And hockey jerseys when it's not."

He almost smiled. "Subtle."

"You're not the only one who knows how to read a field," she said.

Before he could respond, footsteps echoed from the ramp.

Both of their heads turned—slow, controlled—toward the sound.

A man in a suit walked down, talking loudly into his phone. Too loud—overcompensating. His tie was slightly off, his shoes too shiny. Badge clipped to his belt.

"...yeah, level three," the man said into the phone. "No, I see some vehicles, but—"

He glanced at them.

Paused.

Gave them an overly casual nod.

Layla's eyes flicked to Bud's.

He recognized the look.

This is a probe.

The man pivoted, pretending to adjust his jacket, giving them another glance from a slightly different angle. His gaze lingered a half-second too long on Layla's bag.

"Afternoon," he said, hanging up his phone in an exaggerated motion. "Cold down here."

"Better than outside," Bud said, tone neutral.

"True," the man said. He shifted his weight, smile too friendly. "You two here for the summit?"

"Something like that," Layla said.

The man chuckled. "Always 'something like that' in this town."

He was fishing. Casting wide, hoping they'd bite with innocuous small talk that gave away more than it looked like.

He reached into his jacket slowly—hands in full view.

Both Bud and Layla tensed anyway.

The man pulled out a business card and extended it toward Bud. "If you're looking for clearer guidance on some of those oversight questions, my office can help. We're doing a sort of… informal listening tour."

Bud didn't look at the card.

He looked at the man's hand.

No tremor. No tension.

Professional.

"We've got all the oversight we need," Bud said.

"Oh, I doubt that," the man replied lightly. "This place thrives on blind spots."

He stepped closer, insisting on closing the distance by a foot. Not threateningly. Just enough to test boundaries.

Layla shifted so that her body angled slightly in front of Bud's left shoulder—not blocking, but screening.

"Appreciate the offer," she said smoothly. "We're all set."

The man's gaze flicked to her, recalibrating. "And you are…?"

"Nobody," she said. "Which is exactly how I like it."

Something in her tone made him reassess again. His smile faltered—just a millimeter.

He pocketed the card, chuckling. "Well, if you change your mind, I'm easy to find."

"So are some infections," Layla said pleasantly.

Bud almost choked.

The man blinked, recalibrated yet again, and opted for a shallow retreat. "Enjoy the summit."

He walked past them, but Bud noticed how his eyes glanced back in the reflection of a parked car window. Watching their positions. Noting posture. Pattern.

When he reached the stairwell, he paused and looked back once more.

Bud met his gaze head-on.

The man smiled thinly. Gave a mock salute. Then disappeared through the door.

Silence settled again.

"That," Layla said quietly, "was faction three."

"You sure?" Bud asked.

"Yes," she said. "They always send someone who looks like they got dressed by a committee."

Bud let out a breath that might have been a laugh in another life.

"You recognize him?" he asked.

"No," she said. "But I recognize the approach. They want you to feel gently noticed. Not threatened. 'We see you. We're friendly. Talk to us.' That way, when they turn the screws later, they can say you refused polite outreach."

"This is polite?" Bud asked.

"You haven't seen impolite yet," she replied.

He glanced at the stairwell door. "What's our move?"

"Our move," she said, "is to assume every doorway, every elevator, every panel room is potentially compromised. You're not just a random analyst anymore, Bud. You're on a list."

He'd known that. Hearing her say it still made the air feel thinner.

She went on, "The images from your trail camera? I'll have them scrubbed and analyzed by someone who owes me several favors. If

Scarred Man and his team are leaving 47B markers in the metadata, either they're overconfident, or they want someone above them to notice."

"Or both," Bud said.

She nodded. "Either way, we use it."

"How?" he asked.

"First, we map the triple intersection: Maine farms, Somali diaspora ties, and any entity with recurring 47B flags in their internal routing," she said. "From my side, that means pulling logs I'm not supposed to see. From your side, it means getting everything on local movements: land transfers, bank visits, new 'advisors' showing up in the community."

He frowned. "You're turning me into an investigator."

She met his eyes. "You were always an investigator. You just thought you were an analyst."

"When does this turn lethal?" he asked quietly.

"Probably when you get close to proof," she said.

"And what happens before that?"

"Smear campaigns. Accusations. Quiet professional sabotage. 'Ben Day is unstable. His wife is ill. He's compromised.' That sort of thing."

His jaw clenched. "They go near Gena, Layla—"

"They won't have to," Layla cut in. "All they have to do is whisper that the strain at home is affecting your judgment. They'll hint you're exaggerating, paranoid. They'll point to some old PTSD notation in your health file to explain your concerns away."

He stared at her. "You talk like you've seen this before."

"I have," she said softly. "In another state. Around another community. Different names. Same playbook."

"How did it end?" he asked.

She looked away for a moment. "Not cleanly."

He swallowed.

"Why stay in this?" he asked. "You could walk away. Go take a job at some law firm, argue about zoning laws, forget this ever existed."

She almost smiled. "You could shut your mouth, sign whatever they put in front of you, and collect a pension. Why don't you?"

He didn't answer immediately.

Finally: "Because I know what happens when people look away. I've seen it."

"So have I," she said.

They let that sit between them.

After a moment, she straightened, checking the lines of sight again. "We shouldn't linger. Level Three has cameras. Not many. But enough."

"Recording audio?" he asked.

"Probably not," she said. "But don't count on that forever. Tech keeps improving faster than the budgets that pretend not to fund it."

He huffed at that.

She continued, "I'll send you a number later. One-time use. Satellite relay. No GPS. It'll be good for one call—maybe two—before it disappears."

"Who's paying for that?" he asked.

"An old ghost," she said. "Someone who still believes in rules. Even when everyone else doesn't."

"You trust them?" Bud asked.

"I trust their hatred of corruption," she replied. "Sometimes that's enough."

They started walking back toward his rental together, side by side. Two people who looked, to any casual observer, like colleagues leaving a forgettable panel.

At the edge of his parking spot, Layla stopped.

"One last thing," she said.

"Yeah?"

"When Scarred Man told you you'd have to choose whether to pull the trigger… he wasn't being philosophical."

"I know," Bud said.

"He was warning you about Aden," she said. "Men like Aden don't usually get to live in both worlds—family loyalty and operational discipline. Eventually, something has to give. And he knows it."

Bud looked at the empty windshield of his truck for a long moment.

"I owed him once," Bud said quietly. "He doesn't know it. But I do."

"Do you still?" she asked.

He thought of Hassan. Of the missing family. Of the boys in the yard under the eyes of a trail-cam lens.

"No," he said. "I don't."

Layla nodded. "Good. Clarity will keep you alive."

"What keeps you alive?" he asked.

"Preparation," she said. "And a pair of Louboutins."

He almost smiled. "Seems to be working."

"For now," she replied.

He reached for his door handle.

"Layla," he said.

She turned.

"You sure you want to be in this with me?" he asked. "I get the feeling people around me don't have long, quiet careers."

She held his gaze, unflinching. "Ben, you're not dragging me into anything. I've been in this swamp for years. You're just the first one who walked in with his eyes open."

He nodded.

She stepped closer, just enough that her voice dropped to a level only he could hear.

"And one more thing," she said.

"What?"

"If the day comes when you do have to pull that trigger… don't hesitate. Men like Aden count on hesitation. They weaponize it. Don't give him that."

He looked at her, seeing not just the analyst, not just the consultant, but the woman who had chosen to step between him and a probing agent three floors below a summit about "resilience."

"I won't," he said.

"For his sake," she replied, "I hope you're lying."

Then she turned and walked toward the pedestrian exit, disappearing into the light beyond the concrete threshold.

Bud got into his truck, started the engine, and exhaled.

The game had changed again.

He wasn't just a man trying not to drown anymore.

He was a man standing on the shore, watching the tide, ready to move.

And somewhere, between DC and Maine, Aden was doing the same.

CHAPTER NINETEEN
Pressure Points

The trip back from DC to Maine felt shorter—the Embraer faster, the distance compressed by everything waiting for him on the other end. Snow still clung to the shoulders of the highway in dirty ridges, but the main lanes were clear. The sky was a hard, brittle blue that always made the cold feel sharper.

Bud kept one hand on the wheel, the other resting lightly near the gearshift, eyes scanning the road ahead while his mind ran the new playbook.

Three factions. One missing family. One scarred watcher. One boy from another war, now a man moving farmers around like chess pieces. And in the middle of it—him. A USDA analyst with a war notebook and a house in the woods.

He snorted softly. If someone pitched this as a movie, he wouldn't have believed it either.

But he believed in footprints. And SD cards. And photographs taped to his window.

Those didn't care if a story sounded plausible.

About an hour from home, his phone buzzed.

Gena.

He clicked the call through the truck's speaker as the road narrowed and the trees thickened.

"Hey," he said.

"Hey." Her voice was clearer than he expected. Tired, but less brittle. "You back?"

"Just crossed into Maine," he said. "How's Maria's?" "Loud," she said. "In a good way. The boys are thriving on the chaos. Arnie's teaching his cousins slapshots in the driveway. Sly and Maria's oldest are arguing about robotics in the living room."

He pictured it and felt his chest ease a fraction. "Good."

"How's… everything else?" she asked.

"Quiet," he said. "For now."

She didn't believe him. He could hear it. But she didn't challenge him.

"Are you safe?" she asked.

"Right now? Yes."

A pause. "Are you coming down this weekend?"

"Not yet," he said. "I need to get a handle on some things here first. Tie off some threads."

She inhaled slowly. "I hate that you talk like that. Threads. Fields. Handles. Like everything's an operation."

He swallowed. "It's how I see it."

"I know," she said softly. "Just… don't forget there are people at the other end of those threads."

"I won't," he said.

"Say hi to Moose for me," she added, voice smaller now. "He looked confused when we left."

"He'll forgive you," Bud said.

"What about you?" she asked before she could stop herself.

He didn't answer right away.

"I'm not the one who needs forgiving," he said gently.

Silence hummed between them.

"We'll be here a few more days," she said. "Maybe longer, if… if you think that's best."

"I do," he said.

"I figured," she replied.

They said goodbye in that careful way of couples trying not to put too much weight on any single word.

When the call ended, Bud gripped the wheel a little tighter.

He missed them.

That was the part Scarred Man didn't account for. Distance hurt. But it also sharpened.

By the time he pulled onto the road leading to the cabin, his mind was in full operational mode.

First: check the house. Second: check the ridge. Third: start pushing pressure points.

The driveway showed only his own tire tracks from before, now softened by flurries. No new prints near the porch. No unfamiliar depressions near the trees.

Moose barreled out the door as soon as Bud opened it, tail whipping like a metronome set too fast. The dog spun twice around his legs before racing to the truck, sniffing tires as if checking for intruders.

"Doing your rounds too, huh?" Bud murmured, scratching behind his ears.

Inside, the cabin smelled empty—no lingering scents of dinner, no collision of overlapping shampoos and deodorants from upstairs. Just woodsmoke, coffee, and the faint echo of laughter that wasn't there anymore.

He moved through each room systematically, checking windows, doors, closets, the small crawlspace access in the hallway. Nothing out of place. Nothing added.

He checked the hiding spot under the floorboard.

The SD card was still there.

He exhaled slowly.

Then he opened his notebook at the kitchen table and drew three columns, labeling them:

Community | Money | Muscle

Under Community, he wrote: Hassan, Osman, other Somali farms, local NGOs, Hanafi Mosque in Lewiston, language tutors, transport drivers.

Under Money: Grants, banks, "advisors", shell companies, suspicious land buys.

Under Muscle: Scarred Man, Aden's unknown operators, faction three "enforcement" clowns, whoever sent the text.

He stared at the grid.

Everything tied together somewhere.

You just had to find the crosspoints.

He circled one word in the Money column: Bank.

No scam this elaborate operated entirely on cash and goodwill.

Someone was moving funds. Someone was cleaning them. Someone local.

He closed the notebook, grabbed his coat, and headed back out.

* * *

The Androscoggin Community Cooperative Bank didn't look like the kind of place that would host international fraud. It looked like every small-town bank he'd ever seen—brick exterior, faded sign, snow-patched parking lot, a flag out front that had seen too many winters.

He walked in past a bowl of free lollipops and a rack of brochures about mortgage refinancing.

Inside, it was warm and quiet, the kind of stillness that made every footstep sound louder than it should. A teller smiled at him with professional politeness.

"Can I help you?"

"Yes," Bud said. "I'd like to speak with whoever handles agricultural grant disbursements. Community accounts. That sort of thing."

The teller's eyes flickered in maybe-recognition. "Are you with USDA?"

"That's right," he said.

"Just a moment," she replied.

She disappeared through a side door.

Bud scanned the lobby as he waited. Business cards at the counter listed three branch managers. Two he recognized from previous visits. The third was new.

Regional Development Liaison – Gregory Phelps.

He filed that name away.

A few moments later, a man in his late forties with thinning hair and an expensive tie emerged, wearing the kind of smile that said he'd been in customer service long enough to be tired of it but not tired enough to leave.

"Mr. Day, right?" the man said, extending his hand. "I'm Greg Phelps. We've seen your name on a lot of the USDA paperwork."

"Appreciate you making time," Bud said, shaking his hand.

"Of course," Phelps said. "Come on back."

His office was small but neatly arranged—framed photos of him shaking hands with local business owners, a small shelf of finance books, a window that looked out over the parking lot.

Phelps gestured to the chair. "Have a seat."

Bud did.

"How can we help?" Phelps asked, folding his hands on the desk.

"I'm doing a review of certain grant-funded accounts," Bud said. "Specifically immigrant agricultural programs. Somali-founded micro-farms in this region. I thought it'd be simplest to start where the money lands."

Phelps's smile tightened by maybe two millimeters. "Routine audit?"

"Let's call it that," Bud said.

"We're always proud to support new American entrepreneurs," Phelps said smoothly. "Especially in agriculture. Keeps the region vibrant."

"I've been impressed by what some of these families have done," Bud said. "But I've also seen some irregularities. Files being closed without local review. Funds dispersed in unusual patterns."

"That doesn't come from us," Phelps said quickly. "We don't close files. We just host accounts."

"No, you don't close files," Bud agreed. "But you do see who visits, who signs, who withdraws in cash, who moves money internationally."

Phelps' eyes flickered again, just a flash.

"We comply with all federal reporting regulations," he said. "If there was anything suspicious, I'm sure it's been reviewed."

"I'm sure," Bud said. "But sometimes 'suspicious' doesn't trip the automated systems. Sometimes it's more… contextual."

"Contextual," Phelps repeated, buying time. "Can you be more specific?"

Bud leaned back slightly, posture relaxed, gaze steady. "Do you have many walk-ins claiming to be 'program advisors' from DC? People who aren't on the official USDA contact list but say they're there to help families with paperwork?"

Phelps hesitated just long enough.

"No," he said. "Not that I recall."

Bud didn't blink. "That's interesting. Because Osman told me he came here with such an advisor. Said the man was helpful. Knew exactly which forms to fill out. Was very insistent on setting up a second account 'for incidentals.'"

Phelps swallowed. "I see."

"You remember that visit now?" Bud asked.

Phelps exhaled through his nose. "Mr. Day, we service a large number of customers. I don't have immediate recall of every—"

"You do for the ones that could bring federal heat down on you," Bud said calmly.

Silence stretched.

Phelps looked at the window, then back.

"What exactly are you asking me?" he said.

"I'm asking if anyone leaned on you," Bud said. "If anyone from DC, or claiming to be from DC, told you to fast-track specific accounts or not ask specific questions."

"That would be highly irregular," Phelps said.

"That wasn't my question."

A muscle twitched in Phelps' jaw.

"Look," he said finally, voice lower. "We've had… guidance. From time to time. People up the chain saying this program was important, that we should make it accessible. Not create unnecessary friction."

"Names?" Bud asked.

"I don't have them," Phelps said too quickly.

"Try again," Bud said.

Phelps' posture stiffened. "Mr. Day, we're a community bank. We support federal initiatives. We were told Somali farmers needed to be empowered. That this was a priority for regional stability and… public perception."

"By who?" Bud pressed.

"By people with clearance," Phelps said. "They had the right credentials. They mentioned 47B."

Bud went still.

"They said that code out loud?" he asked.

"Yes," Phelps said. "They said it was authorization for expedited handling."

Bud's throat felt dry. "What did they look like?"

"One woman. Dark hair, mid-forties. Very sharp. One younger guy, smoothed-out accent—DC generic. And one man who didn't talk much."

"Tall?" Bud asked quietly. "Scar over his right eyebrow?"

Phelps stared. "You know him?"

"I know his type," Bud said.

Phelps leaned in, voice lowering further. "Mr. Day… off the record? This didn't feel like fraud. It felt like we were being told to stay in our lane. To let the adults handle the messy stuff."

"And you believe them?" Bud asked.

"I believe in not losing my charter," Phelps said.

Bud studied him for a moment. This wasn't a villain. This was a man rationalizing.

"How much cash has moved through the Hassan account in the last ninety days?" Bud asked. "Rough order of magnitude."

Phelps hesitated. "I can't disclose that without—"

"Without a formal request, I know," Bud said. "So consider this a preview. Because that formal request is coming. And when it does, you're going to want to be on the side of 'I quietly cooperated' instead of 'I pretended nothing was wrong.'"

Phelps deflated slightly. "Tens of thousands. Not all at once. But… yes. More than you'd expect from a small farm."

"International transfers?" Bud asked.

"A few," Phelps admitted. "Not directly to Somalia. That would flag. But adjacent routes. Turkey. UAE. Sometimes Canada."

"Shells," Bud said.

"I assumed remittances to family," Phelps said.

"Assume something else," Bud replied.

Phelps rubbed his forehead. "Are we in danger?"

"You?" Bud asked. "Probably not physically. Not unless you start growing a conscience fast enough to make you interesting. The families? Yes."

He stood.

"Lock your systems," Bud said. "Print anything tied to 47B and put it somewhere not connected to your network. And if anyone else comes from DC telling you this is above your pay grade, get their names. Exact spelling."

"Why?" Phelps asked, more like a frightened man than a banker now.

"Because at some point," Bud said, "someone's going to ask you what you knew and when you knew it. And you're going to want receipts."

He left before Phelps could protest.

On his way out of the lobby, he grabbed one of the bank's pens.

Old habit.

You could tell a lot about a man by what he wrote with. You could tell even more about an operation by what it left behind.

* * *

The roads were slicker by late afternoon, snow giving way to a thin veneer of ice in the shady stretches. Bud took his time, scanning the tree line as he drove.

He was halfway between town and home when it happened.

A dark pickup appeared suddenly in his rearview mirror, coming up fast. No headlights. No plates on the front. It closed the distance in seconds, riding his bumper hard.

Bud's fingers tightened on the wheel.

"Okay," he muttered. "Here we go."

He eased off the gas to see if the truck would pass.

It didn't.

Instead, it drew even closer, nudging the envelope of what could be explained as carelessness.

Then it surged forward and tapped his rear bumper.

Just enough to send a message. Not enough to send him into a ditch.

Yet.

Bud's jaw set.

He flicked his signal on and moved slightly toward the shoulder, as if intending to pull over.

The truck responded by swerving outward, darting into the oncoming lane momentarily—no traffic coming—and then back behind him.

Testing.

He took a slow breath.

This stretch of road curved sharply ahead, a narrow S-bend with a shallow drop on one side. If they were going to do something serious, this would be the place.

The truck accelerated again, closing the gap.

Bud made a decision.

They thought they knew this road. They thought they knew him. They were wrong on at least one count.

As he approached the first curve, he tapped his brakes just enough to make his taillights flare, then released.

The truck jinked, adjusting.

At the apex of the bend, Bud did something that would have looked insane to anyone watching:

He accelerated.

Hard.

The truck, expecting him to slow, was caught off-balance. The timing went off. The geometry shifted.

Bud's truck surged forward just as the road curved left, hugging the inside line tighter than he normally would have. The tail slid, caught, then settled.

Behind him, the pursuing truck overcorrected.

Its front end fishtailed outward. Rear wheels caught the icy patch.

Momentum did the rest.

In his side mirror, Bud watched the dark pickup skid sideways, slide into the soft snow at the shoulder, and thump nose-first into the shallow ditch.

It wasn't catastrophic—not at this speed—but it was humiliating.

He didn't stop. Didn't slow. Didn't so much as glance over his shoulder beyond that one mirror check.

He kept driving.

The truck could extract itself or not. If they were professionals, they'd have a tow plan. If they were local muscle, they'd have a long walk home and an expensive repair.

Either way, message received:

He wasn't prey.

Ten minutes later, still riding the edge of adrenaline, he pulled into the cabin driveway.

The house awaited him, quiet and unburned. No fresh footprints. No taped pictures.

For now.

He went inside, closed the door, and leaned his back against it, breathing out slowly.

His hands weren't shaking. That wasn't who he was.

But something inside him had shifted another degree.

They'd made their first overt move on the road.

Next, it would be somewhere closer.

He walked to the table, opened his notebook again, and added one more line under Muscle:

Unknown pickup, dark, no plates. Comfortable with near-miss. Not yet ready for bodies.

Then, beneath it:

They're escalating. So am I.

Moose padded over and sat beside him, pressing his head against Bud's knee.

"Yeah," Bud murmured, rubbing his ears. "I know, buddy."

Outside, the snow began again—light at first, then heavier. It blurred the tire tracks on the main road, softened the sharp edges of the ditch.

In a few hours, there would be no visible sign anything had happened.

But Bud didn't need signs.

He'd been here before. Different continent. Same pattern.

They'd chosen the battlefield.

They'd made their first real move.

Now it was his turn.

CHAPTER TWENTY
The Line in the Snow

By morning the storm had thickened, laying down several inches of powder that softened the land but did nothing to ease the tension that had settled over Bud like a weighted blanket.

He woke before sunrise. Habit. Survival instinct. The sense that he was sleeping in a place someone else had already mapped.

Moose lay curled at the foot of the bed, one ear perked—alert even when resting. The dog sat up as soon as Bud swung his legs over the edge.

"Let's see what the world left us," Bud murmured.

He dressed, layered up, and stepped outside into the pre-dawn hush. The snow was fresh, clean, untouched…

Except for one thing.

Right in the center of the porch, placed with deliberate precision, sat a single item:

A wooden matchbox. Old style. Weathered. The kind you'd find in markets overseas.

He froze—not in fear, but in recognition.

In Somalia, in Kosovo, in every conflict zone he'd worked, matchboxes were used as signaling devices. Contact markers. Warnings. Messages. Sometimes coded. Sometimes painfully literal.

He crouched, careful not to disturb the snow around it.

The box was empty.

Empty meant don't strike the match.

Don't escalate.

Not yet.

Bud's jaw flexed.

Moose padded beside him and growled low in his throat—deep, uneasy, the kind of sound dogs made when they smelled someone who didn't belong.

Bud spoke quietly, "Easy, buddy. We're not reacting blind."

He picked up the matchbox with two fingers and slipped it into his coat pocket. No fingerprints. It was too cold. Whoever left it had stopped by only minutes earlier. The snow wasn't disturbed except for a single half-print near the edge of the step—uncompleted, as if the person had pivoted fast or moved with intentional balance.

A trained step.

Not an amateur.

"Round two," Bud muttered.

He scanned the tree line but saw nothing but darkness and falling flakes.

Still, he felt the eyes.

* * *

Inside, he brewed coffee, stood at the window, and called Layla using another temporary satellite number she'd sent the night before.

She answered on the second ring. "You're calling early."

"I found a matchbox on my porch," he said.

Silence. Then: "Describe it."

He did.

She inhaled. "Empty?"

"Yes."

"That's a stop signal," she said. "Or in some circles… a warning to wait for contact."

"Contact from who?" he asked.

"Aden," she said. "Or the faction pretending to act on his behalf."

"They were on my porch," Bud said.

"That means they're getting bolder," she replied. "And they're testing your response time. Did Moose bark last night?"

"No," Bud said. "This was placed after dawn started."

"Then they wanted you awake when you saw it," she said. "This isn't intimidation. This is choreography."

He rubbed his forehead. "Why me? Why here?"

"Because you're a pressure point," she replied. "A hinge. You connect the farm accounts, the missing family, and a thirty-year-old tie to a man who's now running operations no one can officially acknowledge."

"Aden," Bud said.

"Yes," she replied.

Bud took a slow breath. "He's not friendly. But Scarred Man said he's not hostile to me. Yet."

"'Not hostile' is a temporary condition," Layla said. "It lasts only as long as your existence benefits him."

Bud paced the kitchen. "What about the third faction? The one that sent the fake USDA inspector?"

"They'll escalate next," she said. "They need to maintain dominance. If Aden or Scarred Man's groups are sending subtle messages, faction three will respond with something loud."

"How loud?"

"They like 'accidents,'" Layla said. "Slashed tires. Broken windows. Collisions that don't quite kill. If they get desperate, they send someone to your house while you're gone."

Bud looked around the cabin.

His sanctuary.

His pressure-release valve.

His place between wars.

And it had been breached—first by footprints, then by photographs, now by a matchbox carrying a silent order:

Wait. Let us choose the time.

Not a chance.

"What's my next step?" Bud asked.

"Pressure them back," Layla said. "You mentioned wanting to visit some families. Do it. Not casually. Directly."

Bud nodded. "Start with people tied closest to Hassan?"

"Yes," she said. "Someone knows something. Someone always does."

"I have a lead," Bud said. "Hassan's brother—Mahad. He's been avoiding my calls. He runs a small halal market on the edge of Auburn."

"That's where you start," she said. "But be cautious. If he's withholding information, it's not because he's trying to protect himself. It's because he's trying to protect others."

"Or because he's in deeper," Bud said.

"Both can be true," she said.

He sighed. "After last night, Gena and the boys are staying longer at Maria's."

"That's smart," she said. "But Ben… not forever."

He knew what she meant. This was how marriages cracked—not all at once, but through increments of fear.

"I'll bring them home when the field stabilizes," he said.

"It won't," she said gently. "But I'll help you get it contained."

He paused. "Thank you."

"Don't thank me yet," she replied. "We're climbing into the fireline."

* * *

The drive to Auburn took forty minutes. The halal market sat wedged between a laundromat and a shuttered café. Its windows were fogged from the inside, handwritten signs taped to the glass.

Bud parked across the street and scanned the sidewalk before crossing. A minivan idled nearby, two kids in the back watching something on a tablet. Normal. Calm.

He opened the market door, and a brass bell jingled overhead.

Mahad Hassan stood behind the counter, counting bills and stuffing them into a worn cash drawer. When he saw Bud, his hands stilled.

"Mr. Day," Mahad said. "You found me."

"You've been hard to reach," Bud said softly.

Mahad swallowed. "Sorry. Busy time."

Bud stepped closer. "Mahad, where is your brother?"

Mahad's eyes flickered. "What do you mean?"

"Don't," Bud said. "You know exactly what I mean."

Mahad set both hands on the counter, the way someone plants themselves before they run or break.

"He is… gone," Mahad said.

"Gone where?" Bud asked.

Mahad hesitated, then shook his head. "I cannot say."

"Because you don't know," Bud said. "Or because you do and you're afraid to say it?"

Mahad's throat worked. "If I tell you… more people will come."

"They already came," Bud said. "To my house."

Mahad's eyes widened. "Then you must leave this. You must. This is not your world."

Bud leaned in. "It became my world the moment someone put surveillance photos on my window."

Mahad's face paled. "He should not have done that."

"Who?" Bud pressed.

Mahad's shoulders sagged. "The watcher."

Scarred Man.

Bud didn't let emotion show.

"Mahad," Bud said gently. "Is your brother alive?"

Mahad shut his eyes tight for a long moment.

Finally, in a broken whisper:

"Yes."

Relief hit Bud's chest—but it was thin, brittle.

"Where is he?"

Mahad's lips trembled. "Protected. Moved. Because he saw something he should not have."

"Something at the farm?" Bud asked.

Mahad nodded.

"What did he see?"

Mahad's voice shook. "He saw men meeting at night. Men speaking languages he did not recognize. Men with guns."

"Somali?" Bud asked.

Mahad swallowed. "Some. Not all. Some spoke… Arabic. Some English. One spoke Russian."

Russian?

Bud's skin prickled.

"What were they doing?" he asked.

"Arguing," Mahad said. "About shipments. About routes. About timing. About someone named Aden who 'controls the door.'"

Bud felt the world tilt for a moment.

Mahad's hands gripped the counter tighter. "My brother ran. They saw him. He hid for two days before someone found him. A man with a scar. He said he could keep Hassan safe. That he owed something."

Bud inhaled slowly. Scarred Man had intervened. Not out of mercy—out of calculus.

"Why didn't Hassan come to me?" Bud asked gently.

Mahad looked up with agony in his eyes. "Because he believed coming to you would put you in danger."

Too late.

"Is he safe now?" Bud asked.

Mahad hesitated. "For now."

"Will he be moved again?"

"Maybe," Mahad whispered. "It depends on whether the others find him."

The bell over the door jingled.

Bud turned sharply.

A woman walked in—a mother with a toddler on her hip. She smiled politely, stepped around Bud, and headed for the produce section.

Mahad exhaled in relief.

Bud kept his voice low. "Mahad… are you in danger?"

Mahad's eyes glistened. "All of us are."

He slid something across the counter—an address scribbled on a small card.

"Go here after dark," Mahad whispered. "Someone will meet you. They can tell you more."

"Who?" Bud asked.

Mahad shook his head, terrified. "Don't say their name. Not here."

Bud nodded once and slipped the card into his jacket.

As he turned to leave, Mahad said softly, "Mr. Day… please be careful. They do not fear the police. They do not fear Washington. They fear only each other."

"And me?" Bud asked.

Mahad's voice was barely audible. "They fear what you might become."

* * *

Back at the cabin, late afternoon shadows stretched across the snow.

Moose met him at the door, tail low, senses alert.

Bud stepped inside and stopped dead.

Something was sitting on the kitchen table.

A boar skull.

Clean. Bleached. Perfectly intact.

He scanned the room for entry points. No broken locks. No disturbed snow at the door. No prints near the windows. They'd come in the same way they'd done everything else so far.

Silent. Precise. Measured.

He approached the table and saw a note tucked into the skull's jaw.

Typed. Plain paper. No signature.

STOP TRACKING. STOP ASKING. NEXT TIME IT'S NOT A BOAR.

Bud's pulse slowed.

Not spiked. Slowed.

Moose growled deep and steady.

Bud reached out, pulled the note free, and folded it once. Then he picked up the skull, turning it slowly in his hands.

It wasn't from his land.

Someone had brought it here.

Someone had walked into his home and placed a threat where he ate his meals.

This wasn't subtle anymore.

Bud took three long breaths, then dialed Layla on the secure number.

She answered immediately. "You okay?"

"No," Bud said calmly. "Someone left me a boar skull on my table."

"...Inside the house?" Layla asked, voice tightening.

"Yes."

"Windows?" she asked.

"Untouched," he said. "Snow undisturbed. They found a quiet entry point."

"Faction three," she whispered. "That's their style. Loud message, quiet delivery."

"They want me to stop digging," Bud said.

"That means you're getting close," Layla replied.

Bud ran a thumb along the ridge of the skull. "Mahad gave me an address. Meeting tonight."

"Don't go alone," she warned.

"I always go alone," he said.

"Ben—"

"I'm done reacting," Bud said quietly. "It's their turn."

Layla exhaled softly, a sound halfway between fear and trust.

"Then you're in it now," she whispered.

Bud looked around his cabin.

The silence wasn't comforting anymore.

It was agreement.

"I've been in it," he said. "Now I'm admitting it."

He hung up, holstered the Sig, and set the skull back on the table.

"Alright," he murmured. "Your move forced mine."

Moose sat beside him, ready.

Bud grabbed his coat and stepped into the cold, the last words scarred across the note burning in his mind:

NEXT TIME IT'S NOT A BOAR.

He whispered back into the snow:

"Next time, it's not a warning."

CHAPTER TWENTY-ONE
Night Meeting

By the time the sun slid behind the tree line, the snow had settled into a light, steady fall—enough to blur tracks, not enough to slow anyone determined.

Bud stood at the kitchen sink, staring at the boar skull on the table.

He'd left it there on purpose.

Evidence. Reminder. Fuel.

Moose paced near the door, nails clicking softly on the wood floor, sensing the charge in the air.

"Not tonight," Bud told him. "Guard the house."

Moose looked up, head tilted, ears pricked. He whined once, then padded over to the window, staring out like he expected the woods to answer.

Bud grabbed his coat, hat, gloves. He slipped his Sig into a concealed holster at the small of his back—not his first choice, but this was town, not war. The M14 stayed home. Tonight needed subtlety, not a full manifesto.

He took Mahad's card from his pocket and looked at it again.

Just an address, handwritten in careful script:

Old Foundry Road – Warehouse 7

Nothing else.

"Old Foundry," Bud muttered. "Of course."

Every town had one—a place where rust gathered, kids dared each other to sneak into, and bad deals used the echoing concrete for cover.

He slid the card away and stepped out into the cold.

* * *

The old foundry sat on the edge of an industrial park that hadn't seen real business since the early 2000s. Half the warehouse units were empty, their signage faded; the other half hosted low-rent storage, small-time automotive shops, and businesses that never seemed to have customers but somehow paid rent on time.

Warehouse 7 stood at the far end, its windows boarded over, its loading dock door half-open like a crooked grin. A single security light flickered above the personnel door.

No vehicles out front. No movement. No sound but the soft hiss of falling snow and a distant hum of the highway.

Bud parked two lots away, behind a box truck that looked like it hadn't moved in weeks. He cut the engine, sat for a beat, and listened.

Nothing.

He stepped out, locked the truck, and walked the rest of the way on foot, boots crunching softly over the hardened patches of ice.

Everything about this felt like the setup to an ambush.

He went anyway.

At the corner of the building, he paused and scanned the roofline. No silhouettes. No telltale glints. He checked the loading dock—footprints leading in, faint, recent. One person. Maybe two.

He approached the personnel door and knocked once.

A small metal panel slid open eye-level from the inside. Dark eyes peered out for a half-second, then shut the panel again.

A bolt slid back. The door cracked open.

"Mr. Day," a voice said quietly. "Come inside. Fast."

He stepped through.

The door closed behind him with a heavy clank.

Inside, the warehouse smelled of dust, oil, and something else… cardamom, maybe. A space heater rattled in the corner, fighting a losing battle against the cold. A single string of bare bulbs hung overhead, casting long shadows.

Three people waited for him.

Mahad, in a worn jacket and watchful eyes. An older man with white in his beard and a cane. And a woman in her thirties with a headscarf and arms folded, gaze sharp.

"Thank you for coming," Mahad said, nervous.

"Didn't feel like I had many options," Bud replied.

The older man stepped forward, leaning heavily on his cane. "You must forgive my nephew," he said, accent thick but words precise. "He has the habit of those who survived too much—seeing danger everywhere."

"I'm not sure he's wrong," Bud said.

The man inclined his head slightly in acknowledgment. "I am Sheikh Nur. I lead the small mosque outside Lewiston. You have met some of my people on their farms."

Bud nodded. "I've seen your name on community liaison forms."

"We do not put everything on paper," Nur said. "Paper is… vulnerable."

The woman stepped closer then, studying him. "And I'm Samia. I run the immigrant advocacy group that no one in Augusta likes to invite to their photo ops."

Her tone was cool, edged.

Bud took her in quickly—calm posture, alert eyes, a stack of papers on the crate beside her, rubber-banded and organized.

"You asked to see me," Bud said. "I assume this isn't a social visit."

"No," Samia said. "This is a line in the snow."

She gestured to a folding chair. Another opposite it.

"Sit," she said.

He did.

Mahad remained near the wall, hovering like a witness.

Sheikh Nur settled carefully into a metal chair, wincing as his knee bent.

Samia stayed standing.

"Mr. Day," she said, "you are stirring things that rarely lie quiet. That is dangerous for you. And for us."

"I've noticed," Bud replied. "Someone left a matchbox on my porch this morning. Someone else put a boar skull on my kitchen table."

Mahad made a strangled sound. "The skull?"

"Yes," Bud said. "With a note. 'Next time it's not a boar.'"

Samia's jaw tightened. "That's their style."

"Whose?" Bud asked. "Aden's?"

Sheikh Nur shook his head slowly. "No. Aden uses words, not skulls."

"Then who?" Bud pressed.

Samia exchanged a look with Nur.

"The men who came after Hassan disappeared," Samia said. "Not Somali. Maybe… former soldiers from somewhere else. They speak like people who've spent too much time under commands and not enough time with their own conscience."

"Faction three," Bud murmured.

She looked at him sharply. "You call them factions?"

"What do you call them?" he asked.

"Storms," she said. "They come, they destroy, they move on. If you survive, you rebuild and pray they don't come back."

"And Aden?" Bud asked. "He's not a storm?"

"He's the wind that decides when storms break," Nur said quietly.

Bud studied him. "You know him."

Nur's eyes were weary. "I knew his father."

That landed.

"In Somalia?" Bud asked.

"Yes," Nur said. "And later, when some of our young men were taken by foreign promises. Some promised money. Some promised papers. Some promised a chance to strike back."

"Aden took those promises," Samia said. "And made his own."

Bud's hand curled into a fist on his knee. "He's running operations through your farms. Through these families. Using them as cover."

"Yes," Samia said. "And no."

Bud frowned. "Clarify."

She exhaled. "It started with good intentions. Real grants. Real farms. People needed work. The land needed tending. And someone told us there were programs—USDA, refugee support, state-level subsidies. It was complicated, but with help we navigated it."

"What kind of help?" Bud asked.

"The kind that knows every loophole," she said. "The kind that told us we could get more if we set up separate LLCs. If we registered cousins as employees. If we signed forms we did not fully understand."

"Fraud," Bud said.

"Survival," she shot back. "We weren't trying to steal. We were trying to use a system we didn't build. And then…"

She stopped, jaw clenching.

Nur finished for her. "And then the men with scars arrived."

Bud felt the hairs on the back of his neck stand up.

"Scarred Man?" he asked.

Nur's gaze sharpened. "He visits rarely. He is not careless. When he comes, others move aside."

"He told me he's trying to contain this," Bud said.

Nur gave a humorless laugh. "That is his word. Contain. Not 'fix.' Not 'end.' Just… keep it from spilling where Americans can see."

Bud thought of the matchbox. The skull. The road incident.

Containment didn't feel like what was happening.

"So where does Aden fit?" Bud asked.

Samia leaned forward. "He used to be the boy at the edges. Always listening. Watching. When the militias fought in Mogadishu, he hid on rooftops. When foreign soldiers came, he watched their patterns. You know this type better than I do."

"I do," Bud said quietly.

"Aden learned quickly," she continued. "He saw that the people with power were not always the ones with uniforms. Sometimes they were the ones with money. Or paperwork. Or connections in embassies."

"So he built his own," Bud said.

"Yes," Nur said. "At first he used violence. Then fear. Then… favors."

"Favors like moving the Hassan family?" Bud asked.

Nur nodded slowly. "Hassan called me before he disappeared. He was frightened. He heard men talking about shipments at night, and about… trials."

"Trials?" Bud echoed.

"Test runs," Samia said, interpreting. "Of logistics. Of disruptions. When you want to test a system, you do not start with your main target. You start small."

Bud's stomach sank. "You're telling me the farms are test beds."

"Yes," she said. "Supply chain drills cloaked as 'mistakes.' See how fast regulators respond. How quickly local cops show up. Who asks questions. Who looks away."

"Who tries to fix it," Bud murmured.

"And who takes the money and keeps quiet," Nur added.

Bud thought of Phelps. Of the championship-level denial in his office.

"And where do I fit?" Bud asked. "Why are they paying this much attention to one analyst in Maine?"

"Because you didn't look away," Samia said simply.

"And because Aden knows your face," Nur added.

Bud swallowed.

"He knows mine too," Nur said. "But he sees you as… how did he put it… 'the American who left while I had to stay.'"

Bud's throat went tight. "He said that?"

"To others," Nur said. "Not to me. Not to you. But we hear things."

"So he resents me," Bud said.

"He respects you," Nur corrected. "But respect is not the same as mercy."

Bud exhaled.

"Mahad mentioned men speaking Russian," he said. "You see any sign of that?"

Samia nodded stiffly. "Some of the 'advisors' who came to the farms last year. Always with someone from DC. Never alone. They didn't speak directly to us. They spoke to each other. Russian, I think. Maybe Ukrainian. I don't know."

"The third faction," Bud said.

"The ones with skulls," Nur added quietly.

Bud looked down at his hands. Calloused. Steady.

"What do you want from me?" he asked. "You called this meeting. You risked a lot just by being here. What's the ask?"

Samia's eyes met his, clear and unflinching. "We want you to keep digging."

Mahad made a distressed noise. "Samia—"

"No," she said, not taking her eyes off Bud. "If he stops now, they win. Completely. And they will not leave us alone just because he walks away. They never leave. They only… shift focus."

Bud studied her. "You realize the more I dig, the more they squeeze you, not me."

"That's already happening," she said. "We're past the point of choosing whether there will be pain. Now we choose whether it means something."

Bud's respect for her hardened into something like awe.

"You're asking me to make war on men who've survived it longer than I have," he said.

"We're asking you to shine a light they can't turn off," she replied. "You have access. Channels. Allies."

"Not as many as you think," he said.

"More than us," she said. "We can't walk into Augusta with photos and logs and expect anyone to listen. They write us off as agitators. You show up with numbers and patterns, and suddenly there's a policy brief."

Bud almost smiled. "You think policy briefs stop men like Aden?"

"No," she said. "But they make it harder for his friends to pretend they don't see him."

Nur cleared his throat. "Mr. Day… Aden's people are not the only ones watching you. Some of my community see you, too. The way you visit. The way you listen. Even when you do not understand everything."

"I understand enough," Bud said.

"Then understand this," Nur said. "If you stand up, some of us will stand with you. Quietly. Carefully. But we will not leave you alone."

Mahad finally spoke, voice trembling. "They will come for my family."

"Sheikh will see they are sheltered," Samia said firmly. "And we will move funds quietly if things become too dangerous."

Bud watched them.

It hit him again how unfairly the deck was stacked. These people were already juggling survival, assimilation, prejudice. And now this.

He stood.

"I'm not going to tell you I can fix this," he said. "I can't."

They listened.

"But I can make it harder for them to operate in the dark," he said. "I can pull receipts. I can map movements. I can make enough noise that some senator somewhere gets twitchy."

"And when they push back?" Samia asked.

He thought of the boar skull. The matchbox. The pickup in the ditch.

"Then they learn I don't scare the way they think I do," he said.

Nur studied him for a long moment. "Be careful that your courage does not become their excuse," the old man said softly.

"I'll try," Bud said.

Samia picked up a small folder from the crate and handed it to him.

"Consider this your first payment," she said.

He opened it.

Inside were photocopies of documents—grant forms, LLC registrations, bank statements with account numbers blacked out but routing paths still visible. Someone had highlighted recurring notations:

Int'l Adv. Services LLC 47B – expedited Special Program: Cross-Border Stability Initiative

He frowned. "I've never seen this 'Cross-Border' program on our books."

"That's because it's not on your books," Samia said. "It's on theirs."

"This is faction three's cover," he said.

"At least one of them," she replied.

He looked up. "Where did you get this?"

She smiled humorlessly. "There are some clerks who don't like being lied to. They talk."

"Do they know you passed this on?" he asked.

"No," she said. "And they won't. Unless someone gets sloppy."

He closed the folder carefully. "Thank you."

Mahad shifted nervously. "You should go, Mr. Day. Being here too long… it makes patterns."

"Mahad is right," Nur said. "We picked a meeting place we can walk away from. You must do the same."

Bud nodded.

"One more thing," he said, pausing at the door. "If Aden reaches out directly… if he sends someone… what should I expect?"

Nur's gaze went distant for a moment. "He will not shout. He will not threaten. He will talk to you like an old friend. Like a boy who remembers your face from a different sky."

"And then?" Bud asked.

"Then he will ask you to choose," Nur said. "Between your country and your conscience. Between the rules you swore to uphold and the reality you see."

Bud thought of the trail camera images. The families. The skull on his table.

"Easy choice," he said.

Nur's eyes were sad. "Choices are never easy when both sides hold pieces of the truth."

Bud didn't argue.

Samia stepped closer to him at the door. "They think they know how you'll move," she said. "They're counting on you to follow the same patterns you did overseas. I suggest you disappoint them."

"That's the plan," he said.

He stepped back into the cold, pulling the door shut behind him. The latch clicked, echoing down the empty row of warehouses.

Snow had begun falling harder now, thick flakes swirling in the wind. His boots left fresh prints leading back to the distant shape of his truck.

As he walked, he glanced once at the rooftop lines, the parked cars, the distance to the main road. No movement. No black SUVs. No tall men with scars.

For now.

He drove home with the folder on the passenger seat, its weight out of proportion to the thin stack of paper inside.

At the cabin, he paused before going in.

The boar skull still sat on the table, visible through the window.

He'd been warned.

He'd been pressured.

He'd been threatened.

Now, for the first time, he felt something else:

Backed.

Not by an agency. Not by a senator. Not by a scarred man in the trees.

By people who had the most to lose.

He stepped inside, closed the door, and set the folder next to the skull.

Then he opened his notebook and wrote one clean line:

No more lines in the snow. Time to carve them in stone.

Outside, the wind picked up, rattling the windows.

Somewhere beyond the pines, men like Aden and Scarred Man and the suits from DC adjusted their own plans, responding to shifts they couldn't fully see yet.

Bud didn't know exactly what tomorrow would bring.

But he knew one thing with absolute, bone-deep clarity:

He wasn't just surviving this anymore.

He was in it.

On purpose.

And the men who thought they'd picked the battlefield were about to learn the one lesson he carried from every war he'd ever walked through—

The ground never really belongs to the first man who steps on it.

It belongs to the one who refuses to leave.

CHAPTER TWENTY-TWO
Trigger Words

Bud woke before dawn the next morning to the rhythmic ticking of sleet against the cabin windows, the kind of steady tapping that felt like fingers drumming on glass.

Moose lay near the door, not fully asleep, ears pricking at every sound. He lifted his head when Bud rose, tail thumping once, heavy and cautious.

"Good boy," Bud murmured, rubbing his head. "Long day ahead."

He brewed coffee, sat at the table, and stared at the two objects in front of him:

The boar skull. And Samia's folder.

One was a warning.

The other was a weapon.

He chose the weapon first.

He called Layla using the one-time number. She picked up before it rang twice.

"I figured you'd call early," she said.

"I went to the meeting," Bud said. "Warehouse off Old Foundry."

"Tell me everything."

He did — Nur, Samia, Mahad's confirmation that Hassan was alive but hidden, the Russian-speaking advisors, the Cross-Border paperwork, and the note tucked in the skull.

When he finished, Layla exhaled sharply. "This is worse than I thought."

Bud snorted. "Seems pretty standard from where I'm sitting."

"No," she said. "You don't understand. 'Cross-Border Stability Initiative' isn't a program. It's a label. An internal metadata tag. Not supposed to appear anywhere civilians can access."

"What does it mean?"

"It means someone is using a shadow routing code for money that's supposed to be handled through… higher clearance channels."

"Intel?" Bud asked.

"Not exactly," she said slowly. "More like… interagency slush. Money with no natural home. It gets passed through whatever branch won't ask questions."

"USDA," Bud said.

"Sometimes," she said. "Or Transportation. Or Commerce. Whoever looks the least threatening at the moment."

Bud rubbed his forehead. "And now I've got paperwork connecting that code to a community farm in Maine."

"Yes," Layla said grimly. "And if we file this wrong, they'll cover it up and target you. If we file it right, they'll target us both."

"Always nice having options," Bud muttered.

"We need to be careful," Layla said. "We're not trying to blow the lid off everything. We're trying to pressure one piece at a time."

"Where do we start?" Bud asked.

"With Phelps."

Bud stiffened. "You think we break him?"

"No," she said. "I think we let the system break him for us. We apply pressure where he'll feel it most — from people above him. We don't accuse him. We don't expose him. We make him terrified that someone else will."

"How?"

"We use the documents from Samia to create questions," Layla said. "Official ones. Questions sent to his regional office from an internal audit unit he didn't even know existed. You send the inquiry. I route it through the right email chain."

Bud frowned. "I'm not supposed to have access to internal audit triggers."

"You don't," Layla said. "But I do. And I know someone who owes me enough favors to run this for forty-eight hours before it gets buried."

He considered that. "We do this, Phelps panics. He'll make calls."

"Yes," she said. "And we want to know who he calls."

"He won't call me. He won't call the bank board."

"No," she said. "He'll call the man who told him everything was above his pay grade. He'll call the 47B contact. And… the younger guy you mentioned. The one who didn't belong in Maine."

Bud nodded. "They'll know we're moving."

"Good," Layla said. "They need to feel squeezed too."

"And Aden?" Bud asked.

She hesitated. "Aden won't react to audits. Too bureaucratic. He'll react to something else."

"What?"

"A name," she said softly. "His name."

Bud waited.

"I want to place Aden's name into the official inquiry—not as an accusation. As a point of confusion."

"Confusion?" Bud repeated.

"Yes. You'll request clarification about a consultant named 'Aden,' mentioned in relation to LLC approvals and cross-border codes."

Bud thought it through. "So it looks like a clerical concern."

"Exactly," she said. "Something that wouldn't trigger alarms—unless someone's watching for his name. And trust me, someone is."

"What happens when Aden sees it?" Bud asked.

"He'll know you're not just stumbling around anymore," Layla said. "He'll know you're getting close."

Bud leaned back in his chair. "And he'll reach out."

"Yes," she said. "But on his terms."

"He already warned me," Bud said. "Matchbox, skull, watcher in the woods."

"And that's what scares me," Layla said. "He's being polite. That means he thinks he can recruit you. Or leverage you. Or turn you."

Bud laughed once, cold. "He's wrong."

"I know that," she said. "You know that. But he doesn't know that yet."

Bud stood, pacing slowly.

"And faction three?"

"They're going to react hardest and fastest," Layla said. "Because we're attacking their legitimacy. Their cover identity. Their paperwork."

Bud rubbed his jaw. "You're sure about this?"

"No," she admitted. "But it's the only move that shakes all three trees at once."

Bud turned back toward the table. Toward the skull. "Then let's shake."

"I'll prep the template," she said. "I'll send instructions for where to insert the names, codes, and cross-references. You'll send it through USDA channels before you leave for Augusta."

"Augusta?" Bud asked.

"Yes," she said. "You need to go to the state liaison office. The federal-state pipeline. They log every interagency inquiry into a mid-tier database. Not high enough for spooks, not low enough for interns."

"And that's where Aden's name will appear," Bud said slowly, understanding forming. "In a place scrubbers rarely check."

"Exactly," Layla said. "Once it's logged, someone in faction three will see it. Someone in Scarred Man's group will see it. And Aden… someone will tell him."

Bud exhaled. "And then the board repositions."

"Yes," she said. "The pieces start moving out of the shadows."

He thought for a moment. "After I submit this, what do I do?"

"Go to work," she said simply. "Act normal. Ask local questions. Visit farms. Refresh your patterns. Meanwhile, stay alert. Something will happen."

"Something like what?"

"Contact," she said. "Or retaliation. You've forced a reaction."

Bud didn't respond immediately.

Finally: "Okay."

"One more thing," Layla said. "When Aden reaches out—because he will—do not go alone."

Bud's silence answered for him.

"Ben—"

"I never go alone," he said quietly. "I go with ghosts."

He hung up before she could argue.

Moose looked up at him as if asking what the next war tasted like.

Bud knelt and pressed a hand to the dog's chest. "We're not waiting anymore."

* * *

By noon, he was in Augusta.

The state liaison office sat inside a dull concrete building that every state capital seemed to own one version of—part DMV, part school administrative annex, part forgotten federal afterthought.

He wore his USDA badge, clipped to a clean jacket, and carried a thin binder of "supporting documentation"—none of which would mean anything to anyone who didn't understand the hidden war inside it.

The clerk at the federal intake desk was a young woman with bright eyes and a lanyard covered in enamel pins.

"Hi! How can I help you?"

"I need to file an interagency inquiry," Bud said. "Technical review."

"Oh! Which form?"

Bud handed her the sheet Layla had mocked up. It looked banal. Bureaucratic. Soul-killing.

Perfect camouflage.

The clerk skimmed it. "Agricultural… development… cross-border initiative… consultant identifiers… okay! I can log this."

"Thank you," Bud said.

She typed. Slowly. Cheerfully. Innocently.

Each keystroke pushed a pebble down a mountainside.

When she reached the field for "additional names referenced," Bud watched her cursor hover.

He said, calmly, "Please include the name 'Aden.' A-D-E-N. No last name."

"Oh," she said, blinking. "Uh… okay. Anything else?"

"No," Bud said. "That's enough."

She typed the name. Hit Enter.

Two things happened at once.

A small acknowledgment beep chirped from her computer.

A tiny red light on a phone at her desk blinked—just once.

She didn't notice.

Bud did.

Someone monitored that field.

Someone who knew names not meant to appear in government systems.

The clerk printed a receipt, handed it to him, and wished him a good day.

Bud thanked her and walked out into the hall.

He didn't realize his pulse had accelerated until he stepped into the cold air outside.

The trap was set.

* * *

He reached his truck, opened the door, and slid inside.

His phone buzzed before he even touched the ignition.

Layla.

IT'S BEEN FLAGGED. FASTER THAN EXPECTED. PREPARE.

He typed:

Timeframe?

HOURS, NOT DAYS. LEAVE AUGUSTA IMMEDIATELY. DO NOT GO HOME YET.

He started the engine, shifting into drive.

Another message:

BUD— THE NAME "ADEN" TRIGGERED AN ALERT ON A SECURE LINE. NOT MINE. NOT ANYONE'S I KNOW. SOMEONE HIGHER JUST WOKE UP.

His phone buzzed a final time:

YOU'RE IN THE OPEN NOW. DON'T GET BOXED.

Bud pulled onto the road.

He checked his mirrors.

A sedan appeared behind him.

Then a second.

Neither had followed him from the building.

Neither had been parked nearby when he arrived.

They were too clean. Too smooth. Too familiar in a way his body recognized instantly.

Professional tails.

Faction three.

He didn't speed up.

He didn't brake.

He simply moved into the right lane and whispered:

"Alright. Come find me."

CHAPTER TWENTY-THREE
Signals

The highway out of Augusta ran straight for a good ten miles before it started to twist back into the low hills. Snowbanks leaned in on either side like spectators, gray and crusted where the plows had cut them back. The sky was a flat sheet of winter white.

In the rearview mirror, the sedans stayed where they'd been since he pulled away from the liaison building.

One, the lead shadow, held two car-lengths back in the same lane. The second hung farther behind in the left lane, like a lazy commuter who just happened to be matching his speed.

They were good.

Not perfect.

Good.

Bud let his eyes track them without changing posture, shoulders relaxed, hands light on the wheel. His pulse was steady. The same slow war drum it had always been.

He'd missed this, in a way that made him quietly ashamed.

He clicked his blinker and eased into the left lane behind a tractor-trailer. The sedan closest to him adjusted a fraction late, sliding in behind him with the kind of almost-natural hesitation that came from training and not instinct.

The second sedan drifted into the right lane as if to pass, then stayed exactly abreast of him for four long seconds.

The passenger glanced over.

Not a curious driver. Not annoyed. Just… confirming.

Bud counted silently in his head.

One. Two. Three. Four.

Then the second sedan eased ahead, slipped back into the left lane, and settled in the lead.

Opening a box.

He caught his own reflection in the side window—calm face, more lines than he remembered, eyes that looked less like those of a bureaucrat and more like the kid who'd boarded a transport plane three decades ago.

He tapped the steering wheel once.

"Alright," he murmured. "We play."

His phone buzzed on the console.

He didn't grab it immediately. He waited until the lane straightened, until a billboard gave him an excuse to glance down like any bored driver.

Layla.

THEY'RE USING STATE HIGHWAY CAMS. I'M SEEING MOVEMENT TAGS ON YOUR ROUTE.

He typed with one thumb, the way anyone might respond to a text at seventy miles an hour when they shouldn't:

Two sedans. Professional. Not subtle.

Her reply came fast:

FACTION THREE. THEY WON'T HIT YOU HERE. TOO PUBLIC. THEY'LL TRY TO PUSH YOU SOMEWHERE QUIET.

He watched as the lead sedan's brake lights flared briefly, then dimmed.

An exit sign appeared up ahead:

RIVERBEND – SCENIC OVERLOOK – 1 MILE

Of course.

He could predict the next steps the way he could predict a breakout pattern on the ice.

They'd create an obstruction. Or a "coincidental" lane closure. Or a subtle nudge that made taking the overlook exit feel like the easiest choice.

He had another idea.

He sent one more message:

I'M NOT GOING HOME. I'M GOING HUNTING.

Layla's response:

BEN— DO NOT GO TO YOUR LAND. THAT'S THE FIRST PLACE THEY'LL TRIANGULATE.

He smiled without humor.

WHO SAID ANYTHING ABOUT GOING TO MY LAND?

He killed the screen, set the phone back in the console, and put on his turn signal.

The sedans reacted exactly as he expected.

The one behind him slowed half a beat, then changed lanes to follow.

The one ahead drifted toward the exit lane early, as if the driver had decided at the last second that a scenic overlook sounded nice.

Bud didn't take the exit.

He flicked the signal off at the last possible instant and cut back into the passing lane, sliding past the exit ramp triangle right as the lead sedan committed.

The driver in the first car hesitated—too late to abort. The sedan took the exit alone.

Behind Bud, the second car jerked slightly, caught between following its partner and staying with him. It chose him, swerving back behind his bumper a little too abruptly.

Sloppy.

He smiled.

Divide and measure.

Now he had one to work with, instead of a pair.

He stayed on the highway another couple of miles, then took a random exit toward a strip of nothing—gas station, shuttered diner, an industrial supply yard locked up for the weekend.

The sedan stayed with him.

Good.

He drove past the gas station, ignoring the pumps, and turned right onto a side road that cut behind the supply yard. The asphalt gave way to packed dirt and ice, the kind of access lane truckers used to swing big rigs around.

He didn't speed.

Not yet.

The sedan followed, more committed now, more exposed.

Up ahead, the lane dead-ended into a broad turnaround loop near a locked gate. Chain-link fence. NO TRESPASSING signs. The kind of place cameras looked inward, not outward.

He eased into the loop, letting the truck roll forward until his angle gave him a full view of the road behind.

The sedan slowed.

Stopped just shy of the loop's mouth.

For a long moment, no one moved.

Then the driver's door opened.

A man stepped out, suited, coat open despite the cold. No badge visible, but there was something about him that screamed official—not in a clean, pressed way, but in the casual arrogance of someone who believed the rules bent around his job description.

He kept his hands where Bud could see them.

Showtime.

Bud put the truck in park, cracked his window, and rested his arm casually on the frame. The Sig was a comforting weight at his back.

"You lost?" Bud called.

The man smiled faintly. "Mr. Day?"

"Depends who's asking."

"Someone who would prefer this conversation remain… informal," the man said.

"Informal tends to end badly," Bud replied. "In my experience."

The man took a few steps closer but stayed out of arm's reach. He stopped where the packed snow began to crunch differently—someone who understood distance.

"Nice maneuver back at the overlook," he said. "You're more observant than your file suggests."

Bud raised an eyebrow. "You boys should really stop reading those. They're never accurate."

The man smiled again, thinner. "We're not your enemy, Mr. Day."

Bud snorted. "You followed me out of a federal building with two vehicles. That's not what friends do."

"Friends," the man said, "would invite you to coffee and talk about your concerns. We tried that."

He thought of the guy in the garage at Level Three with the too-bright smile and the business card he never took.

"You call that friendly?" Bud asked.

"Warmer than this," the man said, glancing at the surrounding emptiness. "We like to give people a chance to choose the easy way first."

"Is this the hard way?" Bud asked.

"Depends on how you respond," the man said. "We're aware you filed an inquiry this morning. An unusual one."

"Must be your lucky day," Bud said.

The man's eyes hardened a fraction. "You mentioned a name you don't have clearance to type. That creates… complications."

"Funny thing about names," Bud said. "People tend to have them whether I type them or not."

The man tilted his head slightly. "Mr. Day, I'm going to be direct. You're stepping into compartments you don't belong in. There are operations above your pay grade that involve individuals whose histories you only partly understand."

"Then explain it to me," Bud said. "I'm a quick study."

"That's exactly what concerns us," the man replied.

He took another step forward, lowering his voice.

"You're being used," he said.

Bud almost laughed. "I've heard that before."

"I'm serious," the man said. "These community advocates—you think they handed you those documents because they trust you? They handed them to you so they wouldn't have to stick their own necks out any further. You're a heat shield. If this blows up, they'll call you the unstable veteran who overreacted."

Bud's jaw tightened.

The man saw it and pressed.

"And the people on the other side? Aden? The scarred one? They're using you too. Measuring you. Testing your edges. You're in the middle of a tug-of-war between ghosts. You're going to get torn in half."

"Then tell them to stop pulling," Bud said.

"We would love to," the man said. "That's why we're here. To minimize damage. To keep things… contained."

The word echoed Scarred Man's voice.

Contain.

Bud almost said it aloud.

"But you complicate that," the man continued. "You force things into the light that are not ready to be seen. It makes everyone nervous. Nervous people do… messy things."

"Is this the part where you threaten my family?" Bud asked quietly.

The man didn't flinch. "We don't threaten civilians."

"Says the guy whose friends put a boar skull on my table."

For the first time, something genuine flickered across the man's face. Surprise. Annoyance.

"That was not us," he said.

"Could've fooled me," Bud replied.

The man shook his head. "That was a message from someone with far less patience. Which is why we need you to stop giving them reasons to escalate."

"By doing what?" Bud asked. "Walking away?"

"For now?" the man said. "Yes. You stop visiting farms. You stop calling banks. You stop whispering names into systems you're not supposed to know. Let the adults handle the monsters."

"Adults," Bud repeated, flat. "You mean you."

"Yes," the man said.

Bud let the silence stretch.

He thought of Nur and his cane. Samia and her iron spine. Mahad's shaking hands.

Adults.

"Tell me something," Bud said. "Did your adults create Aden, or just hire him after someone else did the dirty work?"

The man's eyes cooled. "That's irrelevant."

"It's not irrelevant to the people he's positioned around food distribution and land grants," Bud said. "Or the families he moves like chess pieces when they see something they shouldn't."

The man's voice lost any pretense of warmth. "Mr. Day. You're not hearing me. When my people use phrases like 'cross-border stability' and 'community assets,' we mean exactly that. Stability. Preventing chaos. You push too hard and chaos wins."

"You mean chaos stops answering your phone calls," Bud said.

The man sighed. "We're not villains, Mr. Day. We're not saints either. We're the ones who do what needs doing so people like your wife can drive to the grocery store without worrying about car bombs."

Bud's hand curled tighter on the wheel.

"Leave my family out of your mouth," he said softly.

The man raised a hand in vague apology. "Point is, there are... arrangements. Long-term. They keep the worst wolves outside the fence. Aden is part of that arrangement, whether you like it or not."

"He's not a guard dog," Bud said. "He's a wolf you taught to walk on two legs. And now you're surprised he wants a seat at the table."

The man regarded him with something like grudging respect. "You understand more than most."

"That's why you're nervous," Bud said.

"Exactly," the man replied. "So let's not pretend this is about some missing farmer. This is about you. You, specifically, are destabilizing a fragile balance. So I'm going to make this simple."

He took one more step closer, until there was nothing casual about his distance.

"Stop," the man said quietly. "Now. We'll protect your pension. We'll reroute your career to something quiet. Somewhere without pressure. We'll even make sure no one questions your mental health record. You go back to being the stoic hero who shows up to hearings and nods in the right places."

"And if I don't?" Bud asked.

The man straightened. A faint hardness settled over his features like frost. "Then the people who aren't me," he said, "the ones who left that skull in your house? They will decide you are... unmanageable. And they're much less sentimental."

"Sentimental," Bud echoed. "Is that what this is for you?"

"More than it is for them," the man replied. "I respect what you did once. I empathize with what you're trying to do now. But empathy doesn't change physics."

"What physics?" Bud asked.

"Pressure breaks things," the man said simply. "We're offering you a way to reduce it. For you. For your family. For the men and women who have to clean up when zealots start screaming into microphones about programs they don't understand."

Bud looked past him, to the road, the exit sign barely visible in the distance, the world still turning.

He felt an odd clarity settle in.

He'd been in this conversation before. Different language. Different office. Different continent.

Same message:

Walk away. We've got this. Don't ask what "this" is.

He held the man's gaze.

"I saw kids eating dirt in Mogadishu," Bud said quietly. "They called it food because there was nothing else to call it. They'd been promised stability too. I've seen what your balance looks like on the ground."

The man's jaw tightened. "Those are not equivalent situations."

"They're the same song," Bud said. "Different verse."

A beat of silence.

Then the man straightened, posture closing off. "I'm done asking nicely."

"Good," Bud said. "Because I'm done pretending this is a conversation."

He rolled the window up slowly, deliberately, and put the truck in reverse.

The man stepped back, watching him.

Bud backed out of the loop, never taking his eyes off the sedan. When he cleared the curve, he shifted into drive and pulled away at a reasonable speed—no sudden acceleration, no squealing tires.

He didn't give them anything to spin.

In his rearview mirror, the man stood for a moment, then got back into the sedan. The car didn't follow. Not immediately.

They'd made their offer. He'd refused it.

Next move was theirs.

* * *

Ten minutes later, on a straight, empty stretch of two-lane road, his phone buzzed again.

Unknown number.

Not Layla's. Not Gena's. Not anyone in his contacts.

The hair on the back of his neck prickled.

He let it ring twice, then answered on speaker.

"Yeah."

Static for half a second.

Then a voice. Smooth. Unhurried. Familiar in a way that made the years between Mogadishu and Maine vanish.

"Hello, Ben."

He didn't realize he'd stopped breathing until his chest hurt.

"Aden," he said.

"You remember," the voice said, almost pleased.

Bud's hand tightened on the wheel. "You tracked my number."

"I track many things," Aden replied. "Today, you decided to put my name into one of your systems. That was… bold."

"I figured you'd appreciate the clarity," Bud said.

A low chuckle moved through the speaker. "You were always like this. Even then. Direct. Stubborn."

Bud saw two images layered over the snowy road in front of him:

A boy in a ruined city rooftop, watching American helicopters trace flight paths. A man in a trail camera frame, moving through Maine pines like they were his second home.

"They sent someone to talk to you," Aden said. "Eh?"

"Your friends in suits," Bud said. "Yeah. They made their pitch."

"And you declined," Aden said. "Of course you did. That's why I wanted to speak to you myself. Without… intermediaries."

"You could've knocked on my door," Bud said.

"I already did," Aden said. "You did not answer in the way I hoped."

Bud swallowed. "You put a camera on my land."

"I placed eyes where others had already put theirs," Aden said. "My people did not leave you the skull. That was… another hand."

"Your circle's getting crowded," Bud said.

"This is what happens when men who should have retired decide they still deserve to shape the world," Aden said. "They hire other men like me. And men like the scarred one. And men like the one you just met."

"You left out 'men like you,'" Bud said.

Silence hummed for a moment.

"I am not pretending innocence," Aden said. "I have done terrible things for reasons I believed were necessary. Sometimes I was right. Sometimes I was not. But I have never lied to myself about what I am."

"And what's that?" Bud asked.

"A man who remembers you dragging three wounded soldiers away from a fire you did not start," Aden said quietly. "A man who watched you leave food with a dying woman when your orders said to move on. A man who has been waiting a very long time to speak to you again."

Bud's throat felt tight. He gripped the wheel harder.

"You think that buys you anything now?" he asked.

"No," Aden said. "It buys me nothing. But it gives context."

"Context doesn't save the families you're playing with," Bud said.

"You think I enjoy this?" Aden asked. "You think I wanted to move Hassan's children in the middle of the night? To watch Samia weigh every word in case the wrong syllable gets someone killed? You think I do this for pleasure?"

"You do it for power," Bud said.

"I do it because if I do not, someone else will," Aden said, his voice suddenly edged. "Someone with less history. Less… restraint."

"Like your Russian friends?" Bud asked.

Silence again.

Then, more measured: "You've learned more than I expected this quickly."

"You underestimate me," Bud said.

"I always did," Aden admitted. "That was my mistake last time as well."

Bud took a slow breath. "Why are you calling?"

"Because you are at a crossroads," Aden said. "You think this is a story about grants and farms and skulls. It is not. This is about what fills the vacuum when your country's leaders decide they are tired of cleaning certain wounds."

"You're filling a wound?" Bud asked. "You're the infection."

"Perhaps," Aden said. "But infections prevent worse things sometimes. They keep other organisms from taking root. You know this. You saw the chaos in Mogadishu before men like me carved order out of it."

"You carved tribute out of it," Bud said. "And corpses."

"Yes," Aden said simply. "Justice is never clean."

Bud's jaw locked. "You going to lecture me about justice from behind families you're using as shields?"

"I am trying to keep those families alive," Aden said. "You think the men in suits care if they live or die? You saw how they spoke to you. Imagine how they speak to people with no passport."

"So what, Aden?" Bud asked. "You want me to choose you over them? The wolf instead of the leash?"

"I want you to understand the board," Aden said. "So when you make your choice, you make it fully awake."

"You already know," Bud said. "You wouldn't be calling if you thought you had to convince me."

Aden was quiet for a long moment.

Then: "No. I am calling because they will soon decide you are no longer useful. When that happens, I need to know whether I must protect your family… or prepare for you as an adversary."

The matter-of-factness of it hit harder than any threat.

"You talk like you still think we're on the same side," Bud said.

"In another world, we would be," Aden replied. "We are men who have seen too much. Who no longer trust speeches. Who know that stability does not grow out of committees. It grows out of men who are willing to bleed."

Bud didn't answer.

"Tell me something, Ben," Aden said softly. "When you look at the people sending those audits, following you in sedans—do you believe they are more dangerous than me? Or less?"

"Yes," Bud said.

Aden let out a small laugh. "You always did hate trick questions."

Bud's voice dropped. "I believe you're all dangerous. I just haven't decided yet which one of you I'm cutting off first."

Another pause.

"Be careful," Aden murmured. "When you cut ropes in a war, you never know which bridge collapses on you."

Bud swallowed. "Is Hassan alive?"

"Yes," Aden said.

"For how long?" Bud asked.

"That depends," Aden replied, "on how loud you make this, how quickly, and who panics first."

"I want proof," Bud said.

"And I want absolution," Aden replied. "We do not always get what we want."

"Show me something," Bud said. "A photo. A voice."

Aden was silent again, and Bud could hear faint noise on the line—wind, maybe, or distant traffic.

Finally: "Drive to Lewiston. The old train bridge. Half an hour. Walk to the center. Look under the second support beam on the east side. I left something there yesterday."

"You just knew I'd start rattling cages today?" Bud asked.

"I knew they would push you," Aden said. "Men like you don't stay quiet when pushed."

"You going to be there?" Bud asked.

"No," Aden said. "Not yet. This is a gesture. Proof of life, as you say. After that… we will speak again."

"If you're using him as bait—"

"I am using him as leverage," Aden said. "Different word. Same purpose. But I am not lying about his condition. I don't have to. There are enough lies already."

Bud's teeth clenched. "Why warn me about the skull? Why send the scarred one to talk instead of just sending your men?"

"Because we are not at war yet," Aden said quietly. "And I am trying—perhaps foolishly—to avoid making you my enemy."

"You made that choice when you stepped onto my land," Bud said.

"No," Aden said. "I made that choice when I stepped onto yours thirty years ago. The rest has just been… momentum."

The line crackled softly.

"Half an hour, Ben," Aden said. "Train bridge. Bring only your eyes."

The call ended.

Bud stared at the road ahead, the white sky, the tires humming against the asphalt.

Half an hour.

He looked down at the phone.

Layla's last messages stared back.

He typed:

HE CALLED. ADEN.

The dots appeared almost immediately.

WHAT DID HE SAY?

Bud exhaled.

PROOF OF LIFE DROP. LEWISTON TRAIN BRIDGE. 30 MIN.

IF I DON'T CHECK IN AFTER, ASSUME CONTACT ESCALATED.

Layla's response came harsher, faster than usual:

DO NOT GO ALONE.

He almost smiled.

I NEVER DO.

He killed the screen, tightened his grip on the wheel, and took the next exit toward Lewiston, the sound of Aden's voice still lingering in his ears like an echo from another life.

Outside, the snow began again.

Not heavy.

Not yet.

Enough to blur footprints, once more.

Enough to erase tracks—

Unless you knew exactly where to look.

And Bud always had.

CHAPTER TWENTY-FOUR
Proof of Life

Lewiston looked different in winter—quieter, the way industrial towns always get when the snow muffles sound and people move from car to building like ghosts. The Androscoggin River cut through it, dark water flowing beneath thin ice that cracked in the middle where the current still fought.

Bud parked near the abandoned textile mill overlooking the old train bridge, the one that hadn't carried freight in twenty years but still stood solid as a spine of rusted steel.

The sky was the color of used pewter. The air sharp enough to taste.

He stepped out of the truck and listened.

Cars on a distant avenue. A police siren far off. Wind sliding across the river like a blade.

Nothing else.

Moose wasn't with him—he'd left the dog at the cabin. This wasn't a two-creature mission.

He zipped his coat, crossed the lot, and descended the embankment toward the walking path that led to the old bridge. Snow was packed down from foot traffic, but no fresh prints stood out distinctly.

Good.

He didn't want early company.

The bridge itself was old steel lattice—rivets, beams, diagonal braces, all rust-scabbed but strong. Maine winter had a way of preserving old things whether they deserved to survive or not.

As he stepped onto the planks, they creaked. Faintly. Honestly.

He scanned the length of the bridge.

Empty.

Gray.

Cold.

Wind slid through the open trusses, turning each gap into a throat that exhaled.

Halfway across, he paused.

He wasn't alone.

Not in the physical sense—there was no one else on the bridge.

But someone was watching.

He felt it the way he'd felt it in Mogadishu alleys. In Kosovo forests. On rooftops under a burning sun.

A pressure. A gaze. A weight.

He didn't turn his head. Didn't change pace.

He reached the center of the bridge and looked east, toward the old support beams—thick steel cylinders where the deck met the river.

Second beam.

Aden's instructions.

Bud walked to the edge, knelt as if tying his boot, and let his hand fall casually onto the beam's underside.

Cold metal met his fingers.

Then fabric.

A small waterproof pouch, taped to the inside curve with industrial tape—placed where someone would need exact instructions to find it.

He peeled the tape quietly, pocketed the pouch, and rose.

Still not turning toward the watcher.

He walked a few more steps toward the opposite end of the bridge, then stopped as though admiring the river.

He opened the pouch with practiced ease.

A USB drive. And a single photo.

Printed on thick stock. Black-and-white. Unmistakably recent.

Hassan.

Alive. Eyes open. Seated indoors somewhere on a simple mat. A blanket around his shoulders. A timestamp digitally imprinted in the corner.

Three days old.

Bud's throat tightened.

He flipped the photo to check for writing.

A single sentence, in neat, careful English:

He is afraid of the wrong men.

Bud stared at it.

Who were the wrong men?

Faction three? The suits? Aden's rivals? Or something else behind all of them?

Wind whipped the edge of the photo, snapping him back to the present.

He pocketed it and zipped his coat.

Now he needed to leave.

He took three steps toward the western end of the bridge before he stopped again.

The watcher moved.

A flicker in his peripheral vision on the far bank—subtle, intentional, as if the person wanted to be noticed and not noticed at the same time.

Bud didn't face them.

He murmured, voice barely audible beneath the wind: "You going to say hello, or do we play the quiet game?"

Silence.

Then a voice drifted across—low, unamplified, the sound carried by air more than volume.

"You walk like someone who stopped being afraid of falling a long time ago."

Not Aden. Not Scarred Man. Not the man from the sedan.

A new voice.

A woman's.

Calm. Controlled. Not young, not old—mid-range with a tone that suggested global English, not US regional.

Bud didn't turn.

"Friend of Aden's?" he asked.

"No," she answered. "But he knows I'm here."

That wasn't better.

"Are you the one who left the skull on my table?" he asked.

"No," she said. "I don't waste time with theatrics."

He almost smiled.

"Then what do you want?"

"To see what Aden sees," she replied. "To know if you are what he says."

"And what does he say?"

"That you are a man who survived wars without letting the war leak out of you."

Bud exhaled slowly. "He didn't see the years after."

"He saw enough," she said. "And now others want to see more."

"Others," Bud repeated. "Which faction are you? Two? Three?"

"No faction," she said. "And not a ghost. Not tonight."

"Then tell me your name," Bud said.

"No," she said calmly. "Names are promises. We don't have one."

Bud finally turned.

Slowly.

She stood on the opposite bank, fifty yards away, near the end of the bridge—straight posture, dark coat, hair wrapped in a scarf that hid half her face from the wind. The way she planted her feet told him she'd been trained. Not military—different. Precision without pattern.

She didn't wave.

Didn't step forward.

Just watched him.

"Aden wants you alive," she said. "The others want you silent. I want something different."

"And what's that?" Bud asked.

"I want to see which one of them you disappoint first."

He stared at her. "Why?"

"Because that will tell me what kind of man you truly are."

The cold rushed between them.

Bud didn't speak.

She didn't fill the silence.

Finally, she nodded once—barely perceptible—and stepped backward off the path, fading behind a concrete pillar, then into the trees.

Gone.

He didn't chase.

Wouldn't have caught her.

He turned and walked the last stretch of the bridge, keeping his pace even, breathing steady, vision sweeping every angle without looking like it was sweeping.

When he reached the embankment, his phone buzzed.

Layla.

Status??

He typed:

Got proof. Not alone on the bridge. New player. Female. Trained. Not faction 3. Not Aden. Said she was "no faction."

Layla's reply came instantly:

Shit. Describe her—fast.

He summarized.

Layla answered after ten seconds:

That's worse than faction 3. Ben… she sounds like one of the intermediaries.

"Intermediaries?"

His phone buzzed again.

THE PEOPLE WHO BROKER BETWEEN GROUPS. THE ONES WHO DON'T BELONG TO ANY FLAG. THE ONES EVEN SCARRED MAN HATES TO SEE.

Bud looked across the river again.

The bank was empty now.

What do they want? he typed.

Layla answered:

BALANCE. AND IF THEY'RE ACTIVE… THE BOARD JUST DOUBLED IN SIZE.

Bud walked quickly back to the truck, scanning every movement in his periphery.

He slid behind the wheel.

Stopped.

Breathing slow.

Purpose forming.

He sent one more message to Layla:

I have Hassan's photo. File timestamp confirms he's alive. Aden wants a conversation. Intermediary wants a test. Faction 3 already issued a warning. And Scarred Man wants containment.

Layla paused before responding.

Then:

So where does that leave you?

Bud looked at the old bridge through the windshield.

Wind howled across steel. Snow drifted into patterns like runes. And somewhere out there—multiple predators circled the same ground, unsure yet whether he was prey or rival.

He typed:

It leaves me choosing my battlefield. Not theirs.

He started the truck.

As he pulled away, a thought hit him with enough force to stiffen his grip on the wheel:

Aden left the "proof of life" before Bud filed the inquiry.

Before faction three sent their suit.

Before any movement in DC.

Aden didn't prepare for retaliation.

He prepared for engagement.

Which meant—

Aden wasn't reacting.

He was anticipating.

Reading Bud's steps. Mapping his behavior. Knowing—somehow—that Bud wouldn't stay quiet.

This wasn't a surprise to Aden.

This was the beginning.

Bud whispered to the empty truck:

"You've been planning this longer than I've been asking questions."

He drove toward home, the folder beside him, Moose waiting there, and the war he thought he'd outrun now crystallizing around him like frost on old iron.

Before he reached the cabin, one last text came through from Layla:

Ben… Whatever you do next— do NOT do it alone.

He stared at the screen.

Then he turned it over on the seat, face down.

He wasn't ignoring her.

He was choosing his next move.

And he already knew:

Whatever came after this moment—

He would face alone.

For now.

Because the enemy—and the allies—needed to see what he looked like without backup.

CHAPTER TWENTY-FIVE
The Pines Wake Up

Bud's cabin came into view through the thinning trees just as the sun fell behind the ridge. The last orange light landed on the roofline, making the snow glow. From a distance, it looked peaceful again.

That lie lasted about three seconds.

Moose wasn't at the door.

Moose always met him at the door.

Bud's pulse shot up. His hand dropped to the Sig before he even killed the ignition. He stepped out silently, boots crunching deep into the snowpack.

No windows broken. No doors ajar. Cabin looked intact.

Which made everything worse.

He circled to the side of the cabin first—never walking straight into a possible funnel. Approached from the blind corner. Let his eyes adjust.

Tracks.

A cluster of them. Too many to count at first glance. Half-prints from boots with soles designed for grip, not insulation. Not hunters. Not hikers.

Professionals.

The tracks led toward his porch… then veered off.

Into the tree line.

Toward his land.

“Moose,” Bud whispered.

Nothing.

The air had the sickening stillness of a place where something had already gone wrong.

He followed the cluster of boot tracks.

They fanned into three different paths about twenty yards into the pines—flanking routes. Whoever came here hadn’t been improvising. They’d been executing a maneuver.

Bud crouched and touched a print with gloved fingers.

Recent. Edges still crisp. Maybe an hour old.

The Sig felt too small suddenly.

He needed the M14.

He returned to the cabin, moving low, scanning high on approach—trees, roofline, windows. Nothing shifted. No muzzle flash. No silhouette.

Inside, the cabin was exactly as he’d left it.

Except for one thing.

The M14 wasn’t leaning on its stand by the door.

It was on the table.

Someone had handled it. Moved it. Not sloppily—almost respectfully. But the message was unmistakable:

We were inside. We touched your weapon. We could have done worse.

Bud lifted the rifle. Checked the chamber. Clean. No obstructions. Whoever touched it knew not to foul the barrel or compromise the mechanism.

Faction three. Has to be.

Scarred Man wouldn't play this way. Aden wouldn't touch the rifle unless he was planning to leave it as a gift.

This wasn't that.

This was pressure.

He slung the M14, grabbed two mags, and headed back out.

He whistled low for Moose.

Still nothing.

Ten years he'd had that dog. Moose wasn't just a companion—he was an early warning system. If Moose didn't bolt from the cabin now, something had pinned him.

Or scared him into silence.

Bud's breath fogged into the cold air.

He headed deeper into the woods.

* * *

His land stretched across a dozen acres, but the hunting trails split like veins. He knew them blindfolded. So did Moose. The tracks branched often, but the cluster he followed—at least five or six men—had taken the north trail toward the ridge.

Good.

That meant they wanted vantage. Wanted to stage an ambush. Or make a demonstration.

Bud moved low, silent.

One hundred yards. Two hundred.

Then—

A sound.

Half a bark. Cut short.

Bud froze.

Every muscle in his body tightened. He didn't breathe.

Another sound—thin, pained. A whine.

Moose.

Bud swallowed hard, then stepped off the trail and into the undergrowth, moving with deliberate slowness. He placed each foot on solid root, firm earth—no leaves. No twigs.

He reached the old birch stand, dipped behind a trunk, and scanned ahead.

There, near the base of a toppled pine, lay Moose.

Alive.

But injured.

Blood matted his fur near the shoulder. Not a gunshot—Bud knew the look of puncture wounds.

A knife?

A spike?

Trap?

Bud edged closer, making small sounds so Moose wouldn't spook. The dog whimpered weakly, tried to rise, failed.

Bud knelt, pressing a steady hand to Moose's side. "Easy, boy. Easy."

Moose licked his wrist, then flinched.

Bud checked the wound.

Shallow. A warning cut, not intended to kill.

Someone had neutralized Moose without taking his life.

Professionals. Cold ones.

He whispered, "Stay." Then he stood.

They hurt his dog.

They were still on his land.

Now the equation was simple.

Bud slid the M14 off his shoulder and moved forward, following the boot prints that led past the pine, deeper into the ridge trail.

He walked slower now, letting the environment speak.

A branch bent at knee height.

A smear of mud where someone slipped slightly.

Snow displaced behind a boulder.

Movement signs.

They were ahead.

He ascended the ridge, boots silent, heart steady.

Then a voice shattered the quiet:

"STOP RIGHT THERE!"

Bud rolled sideways instinctively, dropping behind a fallen spruce trunk as a man stepped out from behind a cedar twenty yards ahead—rifle raised.

Faction three.

Black winter jacket. Tactical gloves. No insignia. Face clean-shaven and too smooth for this kind of work—new recruit or contractor.

The man called out again, shaking a little, "I said stop!"

Bud didn't respond.

The man stepped closer, sweeping the barrel sloppily. "Mr. Day, we just need to talk—"

Lie. Bad one.

Bud kept silent.

A second man emerged to the right—older, more seasoned. His rifle was held correctly. Eyes scanning. Posture tight.

This was the real threat.

"Ben," the second man said calmly. "We're here to deliver a message."

Bud remained crouched, unseen.

"You made noise in Augusta," the man continued. "Big noise. Our partners want you to understand the stakes."

He motioned with his chin.

The first man reached into his jacket and pulled out something small.

A dog collar.

Moose's collar.

Bud's jaw flexed so hard it hurt.

They'd taken it off him. Left him alive but marked.

The rookie dangled it with a grin meant to intimidate. "Shoulda kept that mutt on a leash, old man."

Two things happened at once:

Bud stood.

The M14 barked.

One shot. One impact.

The rookie spun backward, the collar flying out of his hand as he dropped into the snow with a thud.

The older operative dove sideways behind a rock, returning fire instantly.

Bullets kicked snow off the trunk Bud had just vacated.

Bud dropped low, rolled behind another tree, and listened.

One shooter. One angle. Possible backup further out.

But the older man had the rhythm of someone who'd been in firefights before. He wasn't panicking. Just adjusting.

"Day!" the man called, voice clipped. "That was a mistake!"

Bud fired again, forcing the man lower.

"You think killing my partner solves anything?" the man shouted.

"Wasn't solving anything," Bud muttered. "Just starting."

He crawled to the left, flanking.

"Orders were to warn you," the man continued. "That's all. You escalated this."

Bud fired again, closer this time. The operative cursed, shifting position.

"Stand down!" the man yelled. "We're not trying to kill you!"

Bud snorted quietly.

If they'd wanted him alive, they wouldn't have cut Moose.

He climbed a small knoll, gaining an angle. One careful breath. One slow exhale. He leaned out.

The operative peeked from behind the rock for half a second.

It was enough.

Bud squeezed.

The shot hit home.

The man jerked, then collapsed sideways, rifle slipping.

Silence reclaimed the woods.

Snowfall thickened, settling into a hush.

Bud waited thirty seconds before moving. He approached the younger operative first. Dead. No surprise.

Then the older man. Barely alive. Hit through the shoulder and side.

Bud crouched over him.

The man coughed blood but managed, "We… weren't supposed to kill you."

"You failed on the 'weren't supposed to hurt my dog' part," Bud said coldly.

The man grimaced. "Orders changed… after you filed the inquiry."

"Who changed them?" Bud asked, voice low.

The operative swallowed. "Whitehall."

Bud stiffened. "The suit?"

The man nodded weakly. "He… he said you wouldn't listen. Said you'd push the wrong people. Said once you talked to Aden… you'd be compromised."

Bud's jaw hardened. "Aden didn't compromise me."

The operative laughed weakly. "He compromises everyone."

Bud leaned closer. "Who else is coming?"

The man's eyes rolled slightly. "Two more units… maybe three. Whitehall wants leverage. He wants to… steer the fallout before it gets… federal."

"Too late," Bud said.

The man exhaled shakily. "You… you picked the wrong board."

Bud stood.

"Wrong board picked me."

The man's chest rose, fell, and didn't rise again.

Bud closed his eyes briefly.

Then he stood and scanned the tree line. The air felt heavier. He knew when a firefight was a closed chapter and when it was a prelude. This wasn't cleanup.

This was the opening act.

He retrieved the dog collar from the snow and tightened his fist around it.

"Moose," he whispered, stepping back through the woods.

He reached the injured dog, knelt, and assessed him again. The wound wasn't deep—meant to disable, not kill. Bud tore gauze from his med kit and wrapped it carefully.

"It's okay, boy. We're going to fix this."

Moose licked his wrist weakly.

Bud lifted the dog gently and carried him back toward the cabin.

Halfway there, his phone buzzed.

Layla.

He hit speaker.

"Ben?" Her voice was sharp. Urgent.

"I'm here."

"You didn't check in. I traced the pings from your phone—there were unregistered signals on your land. What happened?"

"Faction three," Bud said. "Warned me with Moose. Didn't end well for them."

"Jesus," she whispered. "How many?"

"Two. Maybe more inbound."

"You need to leave. Now."

Bud looked back at the ridge.

"No," he said quietly. "Not yet."

"Ben, listen to me—"

"They came here to prove I wasn't safe," he said. "They were right."

"Then go to a secure location."

"This is my secure location."

"Not anymore!"

Moose whimpered in his arms.

Bud's voice softened. "They crossed a line, Layla."

"I know," she said. "That's why you need backup. Now."

"No," Bud said. "They need to see I'm not running. Not tonight."

Layla was silent for several seconds.

Then: "What are you going to do?"

Bud glanced toward the cabin, the warm glow through the window, the M14 slung at his back.

What was he going to do?

He answered honestly:

"Reset the balance."

CHAPTER TWENTY-SIX
Resetting the Balance

The cabin lights glowed warm against the deepening dusk, but Bud didn't step inside.

Not yet.

He carried Moose gently up the porch steps and laid him on the rug beside the woodstove. The dog whimpered but relaxed when Bud set a blanket over him. Once Moose was settled, breathing steady, Bud clipped the collar beside him.

A reminder. A promise.

Bud grabbed a bowl of water, set it within reach, then stood.

His hands were steady. His heartbeat calm.

The shift had happened.

He'd crossed into the mode he had spent decades avoiding—the one where emotion narrowed into purpose, where every memory of violence became a precision instrument.

The mode that kept him alive in places where most men died.

He checked Moose's wound one more time, then turned toward the gun rack.

He didn't take the Sig this time.

He took the Colt Carbine —clean, light, suppressed with intention— and four more magazines.

He stepped back outside, closed the cabin door softly, and breathed in the cold air.

The woods no longer felt invaded.

They felt expectant.

* * *

He moved toward the ridge again, but this time, instead of following tracks, he skirted the perimeter of his land, moving parallel to the known approach routes. He knew how professionals behaved after losing a team: They paused. Regrouped. Sent scouts. Measured the threat again.

Whitehall wouldn't rush. He'd send men to analyze what went wrong.

Bud planned to be the thing that went wrong next.

He chose elevated terrain, slipped between two pines, and set up a short overwatch line against a ridge that overlooked the access road.

Five minutes of stillness passed.

Ten.

Then headlights.

A Suburban, not a sedan. Blacked-out windows. Rental plates.

It stopped a hundred yards from Bud's lower trail entrance. Two men got out—bundled in thick jackets, rifles slung low. Their posture was too relaxed for law enforcement, too rigid for civilians.

Contractors.

Faction three's next wave.

Bud watched them walk to the tree line.

"We're supposed to find the bodies," the taller one muttered.

"They're not far," the shorter replied. "Whitehall said Day will move them. He's ex-military—he'll clear traces."

"Shouldn't we wait for the drone feed?"

"Already offline. Someone jammed it."

Bud smiled faintly.

Moose had a collar tracker with a passive-resist transponder. When it registered an impact or sudden movement, it started emitting a broad-spectrum static pulse. Not enough to block major surveillance systems—but enough to disrupt small tactical drones.

Whitehall's mistake was assuming Bud still operated like a bureaucrat.

He whispered, almost to himself, "Resetting the balance."

The two operatives moved deeper into the woods, rifles now raised.

Bud's mind shifted into full tactical mode.

Distance: 80 yards. Wind: negligible. Visibility: adequate. Movement: predictable. Shots: one each.

He inhaled slowly.

Exhaled slower.

At the bottom of his breath, he squeezed the trigger.

The carbine snapped.

The taller contractor dropped instantly.

The second spun, firing blindly. Bud was already moving, rolling left, repositioning behind a large granite slab.

The contractor yelled into a mic clipped to his jacket. "Contact! Contact! Day is—"

Bud fired again.

The man dropped before he finished the sentence.

Silence returned.

No more headlights appeared. No reinforcements surged in.

Whitehall had sent two scouts, not expecting them to die in under thirty seconds.

Bud descended, checked pulses—both gone—and dragged their bodies beneath the fallen spruce, covering them with branches. Not a perfect burial, but enough concealment to buy time.

He searched their pockets. Two radios, encrypted. One burner phone. And a folded piece of paper, sealed in plastic.

He opened it.

Coordinates.

Not in Maine.

In Virginia.

Bud felt the world tilt a fraction.

The location was in Fairfax County off route 28—just three miles from the USDA's east district satellite office.

Whitehall wasn't just running an off-books security detail.

He was running a parallel intelligence channel from inside USDA territory.

He took the phone and the coordinates.

He left the radios.

He returned to the cabin, stepping lightly, scanning with each movement.

Inside, Moose lifted his head, whined softly.

Bud knelt, stroked him gently. "Good boy. You held the line."

Moose's tail thumped weakly.

Bud fed him water, stoked the fire, and checked the wound again. Stable. Not infected. Moose would live, with rest.

Bud stood and dialed Layla.

She answered immediately. "Ben?"

"They sent two more men," he said. "They won't send them again."

"You killed them?" she asked quietly.

"Yes."

A slow exhale through the phone. "Okay. Then we move to the next phase."

"I found something," he said. "Coordinates. Virginia."

"Where exactly?"

He read them aloud.

Layla swore—something in Arabic, sharp and fluid.

"What?" Bud asked.

"That's a logistics hub Whitehall used to supervise before he transferred to Maine oversight. Ben… this ties everything together. USDA isn't the cover. USDA is the transportation mechanism. The money and approvals are a front for moving people and materials."

"And Aden fits in how?" Bud asked.

"He controls the non-domestic end," she said. "He's the interface overseas. The hub in Virginia is the domestic staging point. Maine is the laundering operation."

"And Scarred Man?"

"Cleanup," she said. "Containment. The 'cold' side of the operation."

Bud paced. "The intermediaries?"

"They adjudicate disputes. They keep the deals from collapsing."

"Deals," Bud repeated. "So Aden and Whitehall are both working for someone else."

"Yes," Layla said. "Someone above them. Someone who doesn't appear on any chart."

Bud sat at the table, looking at the skull, the documents, the photo of Hassan.

"They hurt Moose," he said quietly. "Whitehall gave the order. You said you wanted me to work within the system. I did. They escalated."

"We escalate smarter," Layla said. "Not louder."

"Smarter," Bud echoed. "I can do that."

"Good," she said. "Because now we take the fight into their home turf."

Bud paused. Something pulsed at the edge of his awareness.

The figure from the bridge. The woman.

"Layla," he said slowly. "There's another piece."

"Yes?"

"I met someone. On the bridge. A woman. Trained. Said she wasn't faction three. Or Aden's group. Or Scarred Man's."

Layla went quiet.

"You're sure she wasn't undercover FBI? CIA?" Layla asked.

"No."

"You're sure she wasn't state counterintelligence?"

"No."

"Describe her again."

He did.

Layla listened with the breathing pattern of someone connecting dots she didn't want to connect.

"Ben… I need you to listen very carefully," she said. "If she is who I think she is… then the entire operation—Whitehall, Aden, faction networks, finance routes, everything—is under evaluation by a group nobody wants involved."

"What group?" Bud asked.

Layla hesitated.

"The Third Channel," she whispered. "A multinational intelligence arbitration network. They don't 'exist,' not even in classified briefings. They intervene when competing intelligence groups are about to blow up in public."

"Arbitration," Bud repeated. "Like judges."

"No," Layla said. "Like surgeons. They don't care who's guilty. They care what's containable."

Bud exhaled. "She said she wanted to see which faction I disappointed first."

Layla's breathing hitched. "Then you're in the worst possible position."

"Why?"

"Because she thinks you're a wildcard."

"I am," Bud said.

"Ben—wildcards don't survive the Third Channel. They tolerate players who follow the board. Not ones who flip it."

Bud leaned forward. "She's watching. They all are."

"Then don't make a move," Layla urged. "Not until we plan it."

He stared at the M14.

At Moose.

At the skull.

"I'm going to D.C.," he said.

"Ben, NO—"

"They took this to my land," he said. "I'm taking it to theirs."

"You can't walk into their domain without cover—"

"Then give me cover."

Layla paused. Then: "I can get you an appointment. With someone in Intelligence Oversight. Off the books. If you bring the documents from Samia."

"I will."

"And the USB drive?"

He hadn't told her about it yet.

"Bud," Layla said softly. "Do you trust me?"

He swallowed. Looked toward Moose. Toward the woods. Toward the world closing in.

"Yes," he said. "I do."

"Then tell me what Aden gave you."

"A drive," Bud said. "In the pouch with Hassan's photo."

Layla inhaled sharply. "He's giving you leverage. Or bait. Or both."

"He said proof of life," Bud said.

"Open it carefully," she said. "Not on your machine. Not on your network. When you get to D.C., I'll help decode it."

Bud nodded once. "Then what?"

"We expose Whitehall," Layla said. "And force the Third Channel to intervene on our terms—not theirs."

"Can that work?"

"It has to," she said.

Bud unslung the M14, laid it across his lap.

"Be ready," he said. "When we hit D.C., the board won't just shift."

"What then?" she asked.

He looked toward the dark forest, where the operatives had entered and never left.

"It'll flip," he said.

CHAPTER TWENTY-SEVEN
The Belly of the Beast

Bud always hated the drive into D.C. but opted not for the Metro this time.

The traffic. The noise. The political gravity that seemed to drag down every vehicle near the Beltway.

But this time he felt strangely calm.

Leaving Maine's pines behind meant leaving the blood on the snow, the broken bodies, and the men who had hunted him on his own land. It also meant carrying that violence with him—into the place their orders originated.

Moose stayed with Maria, safe and sedated. Gena still believed Bud was reporting early for meetings. The boys were at school.

The peace before a federal storm.

He pulled into an underground garage below a nondescript glass office building in Alexandria—a building nobody looked at twice unless they already knew who used it.

Layla had sent a single line:

P3. Quiet corner. 11:15.

He parked in the dim back row, engine still running.

Layla stepped out from behind a concrete pillar like she'd been carved from shadow.

Dark coat. Hair wrapped. Face calm but sharpened by fear she refused to admit.

He rolled the window down.

"Parking garages again?" he said.

"It's neutral ground," she replied. "Everyone listens to phone lines. Nobody listens to concrete."

She opened the passenger door and slid inside.

"You didn't sleep," she said.

"You tracked my phone again?" Bud asked.

"Your body posture tells me everything I need."

He didn't deny it.

She studied him carefully. "You're colder today."

"They came to my land," Bud said simply. "And they hurt Moose."

Layla's gaze softened. "I'm sorry."

He nodded once.

Then she held out her hand. "The USB."

Bud passed it to her.

She didn't insert it into his truck's system. She pulled a Faraday-shielded tablet from her bag—something not available in normal commercial channels.

"You came prepared," he said.

"For Aden? Always," she replied.

She powered the device, opened a secure analysis partition, and connected the drive.

Lines of raw code scrolled across the screen.

"What am I looking at?" Bud asked.

"That depends," Layla said. "If Aden wants to manipulate us, this will be empty. If he wants to help us, it will contain proof of internal rot. And if he wants to use us, it will be a weapon disguised as truth."

"And which do you expect?"

She exhaled. "All three."

She tapped a command. The screen changed.

Images.

Not of Hassan. Not of Maine.

Bud leaned closer.

They were photos of Whitehall.

Not casual shots. Not public events.

Surveillance-grade images.

Whitehall meeting with men from Faction Three. Whitehall passing envelopes to a Middle Eastern intermediary. Whitehall sitting at a table with a Russian advisor Bud recognized from Samia's description. Whitehall entering a warehouse in Fairfax County—the coordinates Bud found. Whitehall speaking with a senior USDA official Bud had seen testify before Congress last year.

"Jesus," Layla whispered. "He isn't just part of the operation. He's a node."

"Meaning?" Bud asked.

"He coordinates between the domestic laundering division, the logistics hub, and the foreign handlers," she said. "He's the spider at the center."

Bud clenched his jaw. "So Aden wants Whitehall exposed."

"No," Layla corrected gently. "Aden wants Whitehall weakened. There's a difference."

Bud's pulse tightened. "Look at the timestamps. Some of these are years old."

"That's how long this machine has been running," Layla said. "This isn't corruption anymore. This is infrastructure."

Another folder popped open automatically.

Encrypted documents. Internal memos. PDFs with USDA headers—but the language wasn't USDA.

Cross-border logistics. "Stability payments." "Contractor asset redistribution." "Non-standard conflict mediation."

He felt the cold in these files in a way that wasn't physical.

"What is this?" he asked.

Layla's eyes moved over the text quickly, expertly.

"It's a financial trail," she said. "And not just money. Personnel. Movement of individuals across domestic and international lines using agricultural grant infrastructure."

"You mean smuggling?" Bud asked.

"Not just smuggling," she said. "Placement. Positioning. Reallocation of assets and people to maintain geopolitical leverage."

"People," he repeated. "They're moving people."

"Yes," she said. "In both directions."

He sat back.

Everything tightened inside him at once.

"You said USDA was transportation," Bud said.

"It is," Layla said. "Whitehall built an unofficial corridor inside a program meant for rural development. And he hid it in plain sight because nobody audits community farming unless someone like you pokes the wrong corner."

Bud stared at the screen.

"What's this one?" he asked, pointing at a folder marked with cryptic lettering: ATLAS-09B.

Layla opened it.

Inside were profiles.

Faces. Ages. Modified background checks. "Cultural exchange roles."

"Temporary labor assignments." "Community liaison placements."

Every file was Somali.

Every file was processed by the same subsection of USDA. Every file was signed by Whitehall.

Each placement led to a different state.

Maine. Minnesota. Colorado. Ohio. Michigan.

Layla lowered the tablet slowly.

"Ben… this isn't just a local fraud. This is national infrastructure."

Bud felt numb. "What are they doing with these people?"

"Some are legitimate asylum cases," Layla said. "Some are refugees. Some are informants. Some are debtors. Some are—" she paused, choosing the word carefully, "assets."

Bud's voice went cold. "And Aden?"

"He oversees the foreign-side sorting," she said. "He knows which communities will accept resettlement. Which governments will allow quiet transfers. Which factions will tolerate placements. He's a broker."

"So he's part of this machine," Bud said.

"More like a gear," she said. "But an important one."

"Scarred Man?" Bud asked.

"Internal cleaning," she said. "He neutralizes threats. Removes liabilities. Ensures nobody with too much knowledge makes noise."

Bud let that sink in.

"And the third faction? The one who sent the skull and the operatives?"

Layla sighed. "Breakaway network. They want to own the corridor. They think Whitehall is too slow, Aden too independent, and Scarred Man too unpredictable. They want the entire pipeline."

"Pipeline," Bud repeated. "For what?"

"For access," Layla said. "For influence. For leverage. Think of it like… covert supply chain manipulation. Whoever controls population placement controls political weight."

Bud's stomach twisted.

"I don't want to control anything," he said. "I want them out of Maine. Away from the families. Away from Hassan."

Layla touched his arm gently. "This is bigger than Maine now."

He nodded slowly.

Then the tablet chimed.

Another folder decrypted.

This one labeled:

W.H.-RISK-VECTOR-PRIORITY

Layla's breath stopped.

She opened it.

At the top was a memo.

Short. Cold.

SUBJECT: DAY, BENJAMIN U. RISK VECTOR: CRITICAL TERMINATION LEVEL: CONDITIONAL OVERRIDE: AVAILABLE UPON REQUEST

Bud felt the blood drain from his face.

"Whitehall ordered a kill authorization," Layla whispered. "Ben… he filed this a week ago."

Before Bud filed the inquiry. Before Moose was cut. Before the first confrontation.

Whitehall had already flagged him.

He had been a target before he even knew there was a war around him.

The rest of the folder contained internal commentary.

"Day demonstrates atypical resilience." "Possible PTSD exploitable for destabilization." "Family vulnerability: moderate." "Recommend removal if inquiry escalates." "Aden may attempt contact—monitor." "Immediate suppression required if Day approaches federal oversight."

Layla closed the tablet, shaking.

"Ben… they were planning to kill you whether you stepped in or not."

Bud stared ahead at the dim concrete wall of the garage.

Quiet. Still.

But inside, something fixed itself into place.

A line had been crossed. Another line had been revealed. And the final line—the one he would cross next—became inevitable.

"Okay," Bud said softly.

Layla looked up. "Okay?"

"Okay," he repeated. "We take the fight to them."

"We can't do that alone," Layla said. "We need someone inside Oversight. Someone who isn't compromised."

"Do you have someone?" he asked.

She nodded once. "I do. But speaking to them triggers oversight alerts. And Whitehall will know within an hour."

"Let him know," Bud said. "It's time."

Layla swallowed, then pulled out a secure phone. She dialed a number—too many digits for any government directory.

A voice answered.

She said one phrase:

"We have a Daylight breach."

Silence. Then: "Location?"

"Alexandria," she said. "I'm with the subject."

The voice replied, "Extraction or briefing?"

"Briefing," she said. "Immediate."

The voice hesitated.

Then: "Understood. Sending coordinates."

Layla hung up.

"They're rerouting us," she said. "Safe house near Pentagon City."

"Third Channel?" Bud asked.

"No," Layla said. "Oversight. Real Oversight. The kind Whitehall can't threaten."

Bud nodded.

They drove out of the garage and into the D.C. streets.

He checked his mirrors.

Nothing.

He checked again.

Still nothing.

Which only increased his suspicion.

When predators stopped showing up, it was rarely safety.

It was recalibration.

He glanced at Layla.

"What aren't you saying?" he asked.

She looked down at the tablet.

"There was one more file connected to your name," she said quietly.

"Show me."

She opened it.

A single line.

No date. No author. No classification.

Just one sentence:

"Day may become successor if Aden fails."

Bud stared at it.

Layla whispered, "Ben… they're evaluating you."

"Evaluating me for what?" he asked.

But he already knew.

Leadership. Influence. Control.

Someone—maybe Aden, maybe Scarred Man, maybe someone above all of them—saw Bud not as a threat…

…but as a replacement.

Layla's voice broke into his thoughts. "Ben… they're not trying to remove you."

"No," he said slowly. "They're trying to recruit me."

Into the machine. Into the pipeline. Into the shadow board.

And the worst part?

Aden had known that from the beginning.

CHAPTER TWENTY-EIGHT
The Line You Don't Come Back From

The safe house wasn't a house at all.

It was a converted archive suite deep below a federal building near Pentagon City—secured, unmarked, designed for people who didn't want their presence logged. A place that smelled of dry paper, steel, and the faint hum of outdated air handlers.

Bud and Layla descended a narrow staircase, the door locking automatically behind them. A single light illuminated the hall.

Two figures waited inside.

The first: A man in his fifties with white hair cropped tight, wearing a suit that fit him like military armor. Eyes sharp, assessing. The kind that had read too many classified briefings and buried too many secrets.

The second: A woman in a charcoal-gray suit, younger but more intimidating. Not because she looked dangerous— but because she looked calm.

Both carried the stillness of people who lived above the clearance system, not within it.

Layla spoke first. "Ben, this is Deputy Director Rourke." She gestured to the man. "And this is Senior Counsel Dae."

Bud nodded once. "You're Oversight."

Rourke didn't smile. "We're the part of Oversight Whitehall pretends doesn't exist."

Dae stepped forward. "Mr. Day, you've triggered three internal alerts in four days. Federal-level. Cross-agency. Your name is lighting up every quiet channel we keep."

"Well," Bud said, "I've always been an overachiever."

Layla elbowed him lightly, but the ghost of a smile appeared on Dae's face. "You're exactly like she described."

"She?" Bud asked.

"Your therapist," Layla murmured, cheeks heating.

He blinked. "Layla—"

"She didn't violate confidentiality," Dae said. "She described potential risk patterns. Off the record. Before she ever met you at the club. She argued you were more stable than your file implied."

Bud looked at Layla, heart twisting. A different time, a different world, he would've kissed her.

But not here.

Not now.

Rourke stepped forward. "Mr. Day, we need to understand what you intend. Clearly, Whitehall sees you as a threat."

"I saw his file," Bud said. "He signed a termination directive."

Rourke nodded grimly. "We intercepted two contract teams. One in Maine, one en route to Virginia. But Whitehall also contacted a private foreign liaison. Off-books. That complicates the jurisdiction."

"Foreign liaison meaning Aden," Bud said.

Layla stiffened. Rourke froze. Dae's eyes widened.

"You know his name?" Rourke asked quietly.

"He called me," Bud said. "Twice."

Rourke leaned closer. "Aden has not made direct contact with an American national in six years."

"Well," Bud said, "he picked a hell of a time to reconnect."

"What did he tell you?" Dae asked.

Bud recounted everything—Hassan, the bridge, the woman watcher, the USB drive, the factions, Whitehall's off-books corridor.

Silence thickened in the bunker.

Rourke rubbed his temples. "Jesus Christ. He built a pipeline. A population placement corridor."

"And Whitehall's expanding it," Layla said. "Using USDA grants as cover."

Dae turned to Bud. "Do you understand how dangerous it is for you to be holding this evidence?"

"Yes," Bud said. "Which is why I'm giving it to you."

He slid the folder, the photo, and the USB onto the table.

Rourke didn't touch them.

"Mr. Day," he said slowly, "once we take these… there's no going back."

Bud leveled his gaze. "I crossed that line when they hurt my dog."

Layla almost laughed. Almost cried.

Dae exhaled. "Alright. Then we begin formal containment."

She reached for the USB—

The lights flickered.

Buzzed.

Then died.

A generator kicked on instantly, humming low, dim amber emergency lights filling the hall.

Rourke swore. "That's not a malfunction."

Layla whispered, "Someone found us."

Dae pulled out a secure tablet, fingers flying. "External systems breach. Level Three override. They're accessing the building's internal map."

"Whitehall?" Bud asked.

Rourke shook his head. "He doesn't have that kind of access."

Then from down the hall a soft, deliberate footstep.

Then another.

Bud's stomach dropped.

The woman from the bridge stepped into the doorway, scarf lowered, face revealed.

Almond eyes. Unlined features. The composure of someone who had seen every kind of human horror and learned to breathe through it.

Layla froze. "You."

Even Rourke stepped back. Dae kept her posture, but fear flashed in her eyes.

Bud spoke first. "Third Channel."

The woman inclined her head. "Mr. Day."

Rourke stepped forward. "Ma'am, this is a restricted facility."

"It was," she said.

"You don't have jurisdiction here," Dae snapped.

The woman met her gaze. "When borderless conflicts converge, your lines don't apply."

Layla whispered, "Why are you here?"

The woman looked at Bud.

"For him."

Bud lifted his chin. "Explain."

"You have disturbed equilibrium," she said. "Whitehall is reckless. Aden is strategic. Scarred Man is loyal. You…" She stepped closer. "You are unpredictable. You make decisions for reasons not tied to profit or power."

"Is that a problem?" Bud asked.

"It is a variable," she said. "Variables destabilize."

Rourke snapped, "If you're here to take him—"

"I am not here to take him," she said. "I am here to observe the choice he makes."

Dae whispered, "Choice?"

"What choice?" Bud asked.

The woman pointed at the table. "Give that evidence to Oversight, and you expose Whitehall. His network folds. The corridor collapses. But Aden's faction fractures. The spillover will be loud."

She pointed at Bud's chest. "No matter what happens, they will come for you."

Bud's jaw hardened. "Let them."

She stepped closer. "Or…"

"Or what?" Bud asked.

"You give it to Aden."

All oxygen left the room.

Layla stiffened. "No. Absolutely not."

Rourke barked, "That is not an option."

Dae whispered, "She's testing him."

The woman continued calmly, "If Aden receives this, he consolidates power. He ends Whitehall. He neutralizes the third faction. He shuts down the corridor's violent elements. He could restore stability within weeks."

"Stability?" Bud spat. "He's a warlord with a LinkedIn account."

"He is a survivor," she said. "And he respects you. That matters."

Bud's pulse hammered now.

The two paths sprawled before him:

Oversight vs. Aden

Law vs. Shadow order

Exposure vs. Containment

The woman asked softly, "Who do you trust to do less harm?"

Layla stepped in front of Bud, voice shaking: "Ben. Look at me. I know who you are. You're not a man who hands power to predators."

He didn't look away.

Dae added, "If you give this to Aden, you give him legitimacy."

Rourke added, "And you paint a target on every person he touches."

The woman's eyes didn't move. "He will do what must be done. Quickly. Quietly. Without bureaucratic delay."

"Which means killing," Layla snapped.

"Killing the right people," the woman replied.

Bud's vision narrowed.

This was the line.

This was the moment.

He hadn't believed it would ever come to this—choosing between imperfect guardians and precise devils.

He closed his eyes. Saw Moose bleeding. Saw Samia trembling. Saw the boys on the ice. Saw Hassan in a blanket. Saw his younger self in Mogadishu—dragging wounded through dirt because no one else could get there fast enough.

And then—

A clarity he hadn't felt in decades.

He opened his eyes.

"I choose," he said quietly, "neither."

The woman blinked. "That is not—"

Bud grabbed the USB, broke it in half with a violent snap, and tossed the pieces across the floor.

Everyone froze.

Even the Third Channel woman.

Bud reached into his jacket, pulled out his phone, and tapped SEND on a queued message.

Layla gasped when she saw who it was addressed to:

A federal reporter. Investigative. Untouchable.

Bud looked at the officials.

"At this point," he said, "sunlight is safer than shadows."

Rourke stared at him. "Do you realize what you've done?"

"Yes," Bud said. "I removed the board."

Dae whispered, horrified, "You've made it public."

Bud nodded. "If they kill me now, I become proof."

The Third Channel woman's expression changed— for the first time to something like genuine surprise.

"You've created a third path," she said softly.

"No," Bud said. "I created the only one that doesn't give power to murderers."

Layla's hands trembled. "This… this will trigger a cartel of federal reactions."

"It'll trigger everything," Rourke said. "Political. Criminal. Diplomatic. You've turned a covert corridor into national news."

Dae whispered, "Ben Day just detonated Washington."

Bud exhaled.

Finally— the weight lifted.

Not gone. Never gone. But shared.

Layla stepped close, her voice shaking. "Ben… this means they'll hunt you harder."

Bud nodded. "Good."

"Good?" she whispered.

"They won't waste time hurting families," Bud said. "Or cutting dogs. Or playing with immigrants on back roads. They'll aim at me. Finally. Cleanly."

The woman from the Third Channel studied him.

"You have disappointed every faction," she said softly. "All at once."

Bud nodded.

"Good," he repeated.

"Explain," she said.

"Because," Bud said, "it means I'm finally on my own side."

She nodded once—an acknowledgment he hadn't expected.

"You will see me again," she said.

"Not if I see you first," Bud replied.

She almost smiled.

Then she stepped backward—

—and vanished into the hallway as the emergency lights flickered again.

Layla exhaled, covering her mouth. "Ben… what happens now?"

Bud looked at the stairwell.

Then at his hands.

Then at the world opening in front of him—messy, violent, uncertain.

"Now?" he said quietly.

"We go find Hassan."

"And after that?"

Bud met her eyes. Gentle. Tired. Certain.

"After that," he said, "I go where this all started."

Layla swallowed. "Somalia?"

Bud nodded.

"Somalia," he said.

"Why?" she asked softly.

"Because Aden didn't just wake up one day and build a corridor," he said. "Someone taught him. Someone funded him. Someone trained Scarred Man. Someone controlled Whitehall. Someone built this board long before I stepped on it."

He picked up the folder of Samia's documents, the photo of Hassan, and the broken USB.

"This wasn't one conspiracy," he said. "It was a generation."

Layla stepped closer. "And you're going to bring it down?"

Bud walked toward the stairs as alarms climbed through the structure—shrill, urgent, converging like hounds on a scent.

He didn't hurry.

Predators moved fast.

Hunters moved steady.

Every faction would react now—Whitehall, Aden, the breakaways, the intermediaries whose names no badge carried. He had torn the lid off a machine no one had ever meant to expose.

Good.

Let them scramble.

Let them panic.

Let them come.

He reached the stairwell door and pushed it open. Cold air surged down the concrete shaft, carrying the city's fear and fury in equal measure.

Bud stepped upward into it.

This wasn't an ending.

It was the moment before the rifle cracks.

The breath before the blast.

The second the hunter finally sees the shape of the thing stalking him.

Bud welcomed it.

He'd been many things in his life—airman, rescuer, analyst, husband, sinner.

But he had never stopped being the man who walked toward the fight.

And tonight, the whole world had finally decided to walk back toward him.

Published by

SloariX Media

www.media.sloarix.com

www.ingramcontent.com/pod-product-compliance
Lightning Source LLC
LaVergne TN
LVHW100521110826
845146LV00002B/727

* 9 7 9 8 9 9 4 7 6 0 8 0 2 *